The ... of Death

DEAN EDWARDS

A Black Horse Western

ROBERT HALE · LONDON

© Dean Edwards 1999
First published in Great Britain 1999

ISBN 0 7090 6505 1

Robert Hale Limited
Clerkenwell House
Clerkenwell Green
London EC1R 0HT

Photoset in North Wales by
Derek Doyle & Associates, Mold, Flintshire.
Printed and bound in Great Britain by
WBC Book Manufacturers Limited, Bridgend

Dedicated to
the memory of my uncle,
Eddie Phillips

ONE

The trail seemed to lead south. That was the way it looked to the lone hunter. It was hard to tell in the afternoon sun and the swirling heat that rose from the ground into the rider's eyes. It had been a long chase which should have ended long ago and would have, had it not been for the gritty determination of the lone man in the tall saddle. It had taken almost two long years to reach this point and the man with the dry cracked lips and empty canteen sat wondering how much longer he could continue to follow this trail. This damn trail. It had started in Montana, and now he was staring across the wide desert that led into Mexico. There were no borders here, no neat signs in the sand that let travellers know where they were. Here there was only mile after mile of distance that appeared to stretch as far as the eye could see in the shimmering heat-haze.

The four riders' tracks were being blown away

with every beat of his tired heart as the warm breeze drifted across the flat mesa. Soon they would be gone. He had to try and work out exactly where they were heading so that he could locate them again, if he would ever locate them again. Dust filled his mouth and coated his teeth as he stared into the distance. Not even birds flew out there, he noticed. This was a land that God had not yet reached. Only the Devil reigned out there in the merciless heat.

Bob Cooper lifted his empty canteen off the saddlehorn and shook it once more, then returned it to its position alongside his long rope. He sat watching the haze move the scenery before his eyes and cursed this desert for its habit of mocking him. It was no ordinary place; this had to be the closest any man could ride on earth before feeling the heat of Hell burning his skin.

Bob Cooper was no ordinary man. No ordinary hunter. He was a man who sought justice and the band of scum that had destroyed his life two years earlier in the hills of Montana. His was a mission to catch up with the five men who had raided his small ranch and killed his young wife and child. He did not know the names of his prey, only the trail that they left behind them; only the death that they dished out along the way that he had discovered as he done with his own family. Whoever these folks were they were not human, as he understood the word. These were animals. Mad animals. Cooper had already caught up with one of the bandits and sent the varmint to his Maker. That had been eight months earlier when he was still fresh and filled with strength. Now with four of the killers still ahead of him, he knew that he was merely a shell of his former self.

Only willpower drove him on now, willpower and a pure heart that knew it had to continue.

Nightmares still haunted his every sleeping moment and Bob Cooper had started to dread closing his sore, burning eyes at night. It was no normal man who feared sleep or the dreams that always followed. He had ridden far away from any normal life and now was nothing more than a hunter. Sleep once offered him rest, but that was long ago before the slaughter of his loved ones. Now he feared closing his eyes in case he saw the images that had destroyed him, his faith.

Cooper drew up his reins in his tired hands and spurred his horse ahead so that the creature could once more begin another long walk through even more sand. The horse was in better shape than its master, as the rider had given the last of the water from the canteen to the beast that very morning. Now the rider just sat slumped in the saddle, half dead from the long journey, and yet he somehow held onto the leather reins in his dry hands. If there was water out there, the beast would find it, Cooper concluded.

Those he sought with such hatred in his soul knew that they were being chased. Those he sought must have deliberately led him into this wilderness knowing that he would follow. Was this their final attempt to get rid of the man who haunted their every waking moment? Always a couple of days behind the killers. Always there.

Cooper felt the skin peeling from his face as he rode. Even his Stetson offered no protection from the sun as it reflected off the white sand beneath the horse's hooves. Mile after mile he rode, more dead than alive as the horse walked. The trail was lost but that was of no concern to the lone hunter as he just hung onto the saddlehorn trying not to give in to death. He had a mission that was almost holy in its simplicity: he had to find the last four killers and administer justice.

The law had been of no use. Two years earlier the law had raised its hands and covered its legal eyes. Send out a posse after the killers of a rancher's family? What would that cost? They were only settlers after all.

Bob Cooper had waited too long for the law to act and his waiting had been in vain. Selling everything he owned, he had bought a fine horse and a fine gun, a Winchester, and had filled his saddle-bags with his remaining wealth. It had totalled a mere $400 in gold coins which now was mostly gone. Two years of hunting the men had brought him down to his last $20.

Perhaps if it all ended here as he hung onto his horse and ventured deeper and deeper into the burning desert, it would be better. His mind played with every thought that drifted into his confused state. Death did seem a very real alternative to his continuing on and on and on. Cooper was no quitter though.

Any other man would have fallen into the burning sand and been ripped apart by buzzards days ago. Cooper was made of stronger stuff. His was a soul that would not quit until he had no say in the matter.

Pulling hard against his tired hands, the horse began to quicken its pace beneath his saddle-sore butt. Bob Cooper found himself being jogged back into consciousness as the steed started to trot, then canter through the arid sand.

Suddenly even the lone hunter, as he gripped onto the galloping horse, could smell the freshness in his sand-filled nostrils.

Water.

The horse was running toward water.

Bob Cooper rubbed his face with his free hand and squinted at the desert ahead. All his eyes could see was the mirage of swirling vapours that filled the horizon. The heat-haze made nothing seem real but the smell was real enough. If he had any doubts, the running horse between his legs soon dispelled them.

If there was just one drop of water out there, his thirsty horse would locate it.

'Water,' Bob Cooper said, through gritted teeth as he hung onto his reins. The salt of his tears burned a trail down his dry, peeling face.

TWO

The horse drank more water than was good for it, but Bob Cooper had his belly full too. This was the end of a long desperate ride that Cooper had felt might be his last. This was new territory for the hunter. This was a land that he had never seen before. He had heard stories of this place, but none of the stories came anywhere close to how bad it truly was. White sand and little cover to keep the blistering sun off his back made every moment here a fight with death itself. Here, even the vultures seemed to have disappeared. Bob Cooper sat quietly beneath the leafy trees that surrounded the small water-hole whilst his horse wandered around free of its saddle eating its fill of the fresh juicy grass that pervaded the area.

Hunger was now starting to rear its painful head inside the man's aching stomach. Bob Cooper would have eaten if he had had anything left in his saddle-bags worth eating. He rested

13

against the saddle and simply watched his horse graze and wished his hunger could be so easily satisfied. The small drinking hole beneath a group of large boulders was a miracle that he was thankful for. The handful of trees in the area must identify the only source of fresh water for many miles, Cooper concluded. That one thought occupied the hunter's mind as he rested. He had only one canteen and that was the limit of how much of this life-saving liquid he would be able to take with him when he continued his journey. The fear of not finding another water-hole overwhelmed the young man as he rested, holding his painful guts tightly.

Then he heard a noise out in the hot, blazing desert. It was a noise that caused the man to draw his Colt .45 and hold it to his chest. His horse, too, heard something and raised its head, pricking its ears.

Rolling over onto his belly, Cooper pulled the hammer back with his thumb until it clicked into position. He lay staring through the thick foot-tall grass as the sound grew ever closer.

Then he saw it. A fat wild boar with tusks that could rip a puma to shreds was shuffling towards him at a brisk pace. Bob Cooper could feel his heart beating wildly inside his worn shirt as he lay flat, staring ahead.

The animal wanted a drink and was heading for the water-hole to satisfy his thirst.

The Valley of Death

All Bob Cooper had to do was hold his aim and hit the target. A head shot seemed the obvious target although he wondered how thick the creature's skull might be. Closing his left eye he stared down the length of the gun and used the sight on the tip of the barrel to find the head of the wild pig as it approached. The animal seemed to bounce up and down as if its legs had springs inside them. This was no easy shot for a man whose vision was long past its best. Sand had scarred his face for weeks as he had ridden deeper and deeper into this dry wasteland. How close should he allow this critter to get to him before he fired? What if his shot only wounded the animal? Did he have enough strength to get out of the way of a wounded boar?

Bob Cooper's mind was weary with hunger as he aimed at the large wild animal. He squeezed the trigger and lost sight of the beast as the cloud of smoke left his pistol. Getting to his knees to get a better look, Cooper's face went white as he saw the boar charging straight at him.

Rolling to one side he fired again and then again at the animal that seemed very angry and unwilling to die easily or without a fight. The boar crashed into the man sending him falling backwards onto his back. As his eyes saw the tusks above him, he fired again into the boar's open mouth. This final shot did the trick.

Suddenly, Bob Cooper realized, as he lay upon his back, the body of the wild pig was lying on his legs. It took several minutes before he found the strength to crawl from beneath its incredible weight.

He got to his feet and stepped over the dead creature and staggered to his saddle-bags, pulled out a bag of salt and a small pan. He glanced at his horse who was once again grazing. His hands were still shaking as the sudden horror of the charging creature filled his thoughts.

'Roast pig for dinner,' he mumbled to himself, as he tried to reclaim his nerves. 'I reckon it's bacon for breakfast, too.'

As he pulled out a long knife from the saddle-bag and slowly walked back to the dead animal, his expression was now happier as he thought about the meals this beast would provide. Kneeling down beside the animal he remembered times when he had butchered stock for the family table. His child's face drifted into his mind.

Without knowing why he started to say grace.

THREE

The four dust-covered riders drew up their mounts before the water trough outside an old deserted adobe. By the state of the place, it had not been occupied for a long time, but offered the tired riders shelter for the coming night. None of the weatherbeaten riders dismounted as their thirsty horses drank. The four men just sat and watched the drifting sand behind them blowing away their trail.

Jake Cass had once been a major with the Confederate Army before turning renegade with a handful of his men after the surrender. Their war had not ended. They had learned to kill and they saw no reason to stop. All that remained from his days of glory were his grey hat and his sabre that hung from its sash at his side. Cass was a man who never surrendered even if his army did so. To him the art of killing and taking what he wanted had become a habit he liked. He had killed the young wife of the man who was

17

hunting him. Cass had taken her first then allowed his men to emulate his depravity. The child had simply been another notch upon his gun handle. Now down to a mere three men, he was running out of places to pillage. Mexico offered a final attempt at finding fresh pickings.

Joe Watkins, Cy Holmes and Fred Green were all thinking the same thing. Had they at long last seen the back of Bob Cooper?

None of them had even heard of the rancher before they had raided his Montana ranch two years earlier. Yet in those two years the man had made his presence known to them. He had picked off Sam Jones over half a year before when the ex-sergeant had broken ranks and left their tightly grouped band. They knew that Cooper was a man on a mission. Only death would stop him hunting them.

'Reckon that he's quit trailing us, Major?' Watkins leaned across to ask the tight-lipped man who sat motionless in his saddle.

Cass glanced at the shimmering desert behind them and gave a deep thoughtful sigh. 'He'll never quit, Joe.'

'We ought to quit running and face the bastard,' Holmes chipped in, stepping off his tall grey mare and moving around to his leader's side.

Cass looked down at the fair-haired man. 'How can we fight a ghost, Cy?'

'What ya mean?' Holmes removed his battered hat and beat the sand from it against his leg.

'We ain't never seen the man's face,' Cass brooded, clutching the handle of his sabre. 'How can we fight a man we don't even know? It would be like trying to kill the wind for blowing.'

'Why does he keep on coming?' Fred Green chipped in.

'Why does a fox know he has to kill a chicken?' Cass sighed.

'It's been two damn' years, Major,' Holmes repeated. 'How long have we got to keep running?'

'We ain't running,' Cass snapped, 'we are heading south so we can get some fresh pickings.'

'We ought to try and fight it out with the critter, Major,' Watkins said, watching the cold-eyed man who had led them for so many years. 'It's time to make a stand.'

'You might be right,' Cass sighed.

'Then are we gonna stop here and fight the critter?'

Cass dismounted and moved away from his men. His eyes squinted at the wide prairie before him. The sun was almost ready to set and the heat was starting to disappear.

'How can you stop a ghost?' the man mumbled again.

Now all four men were off their horses. The

stars were out above their heads as they removed the saddles from their horses and entered the deserted adobe. The men were all worried that their leader was beginning to believe that they were not being hunted by a living man but the phantom of their past deeds.

FOUR

The morning sun had only just risen above the horizon when Bob Cooper awoke from his shallow sleep. The long shadows that traced across his bedroll toward the water-hole chilled his bones as he listened to the approaching footsteps. There were at least a half-dozen of them, Cooper figured, as he lay watching the shadows getting larger. He slid his .45 from its holster next to him under the rough blanket and lay still and silent The smoke that drifted down to him was of a variety of cigar he was unused to. Its aroma was pungent and strong.

'Get up, *gringo*,' the very Latin voice ordered.

Cooper rolled over and tried to focus. The low sun was behind the men and blinded him. 'Howdy.'

'Rise to your feet,' another voice said. This time he heard the sound of a pistol hammer being cocked.

Bob Cooper let go of his gun and left it with

the gunbelt beneath the blanket as he slowly got to his feet. Standing in his stockinged feet he ran both hands through his hair and forced it off his face. The sight before him was gradually starting to come into focus as he waited for the next command.

'What you doing here?' a third voice asked.

Cooper watched all six of the sombrero wearing men in their flared pants as they slowly surrounded him.

'Just passing through,' he answered.

'Where you heading, *amigo*?' the tallest of the men asked.

'I have no idea, friend,' Cooper shrugged.

Then four of the men seemed to be more interested in the camp-fire and the remains of the roasted pig that lay amid the ashes. They knelt down and started cutting off chunks of the meat.

'You like eating pig?' Cooper asked, with a smile on his face.

'You like living?' the tallest Mexican grinned.

Cooper nodded and rubbed his face thoughtfully. 'I'm chasing some white men. Killers.'

The tall man chewed on a slab of the pork as his eyes studied the hunter. 'Bad men?'

'Real bad,' Cooper replied.

'We know of these men.' The taller man rubbed his greasy mouth with his shirt sleeve. 'They go south. You are chasing these men?'

Cooper chewed his lip. 'Yeah, I've been chasing

them for the last two damn' years.'

'You are most fortunate that we found you before you continued your journey, my friend,' the black-eyed man said, as he picked the pork from his teeth.

'How come?' Cooper looked around for his boots.

'Because the men you are after have ridden into what we call the desert of ghosts and that leads to Valley of Death.' The Mexican looked deadly serious. 'A most evil place for the unprepared such as yourself. If they venture into the valley itself, they will not return.'

Cooper suddenly became aware that this place was even more dangerous than he had thought. 'Valley of Death?'

'Do not laugh, *amigo*,' the Mexican warned. 'Even the Apache will not enter that place. It is bad medicine.'

Cooper's eyes locked on to the taller man in the sombrero. 'I guess you've got a name. What is it?'

'My name is Juan Cortez.' The tallest of the Mexicans gave a slight bow as he introduced himself. 'These are my men. What do they call you, *amigo*?'

'Cooper.'

'Cooper. A strong name.' Cortez chewed. 'What these men do that make you follow them through this country?'

Bob Cooper's face went sallow. 'They killed my wife and child.'

Juan Cortez turned and spoke to his men in Spanish. When he had finished, each and every one of the men's faces seemed somehow different. Now there was sympathy mixed with respect in their eyes.

'You want company, *amigo*?' Cortez asked, as he finished his meat.

Bob Cooper was surprised by the question. He shrugged, as he thought about it for a while. He had been alone on his quest for so long that he was uneasy in the company of fellow humans.

'You do not have to answer now,' Cortez grinned. 'First you come with us.'

'Where you boys heading?' Cooper accepted the long cigar that he was offered and bit the end off it before accepting a light.

'To my rancho.' Cortez pointed toward the sun. 'It is only an hour's ride, but it is a million miles away from this place.'

'I'm heading after the killers.' Bob Cooper's face went grim, as he thought about the men that he had trailed for so long. 'I ride alone.'

Juan Cortez stepped forward and placed a hand upon the man's shoulder. 'Come with us and you will have a chance of catching up with them: try to go alone from here and the desert, she will kill you.'

Cooper raised his cigar to his mouth and

sucked on the strong smoke. 'How?'

'There is no water for many days.' Cortez's smile turned to a serious frown. 'Come with us and we will help you.'

'Why would you wanna help me, Cortez?' Cooper repeated his question.

'You require water. Much water.' The tall man chewed on the cigar and tilted his head so that the sun filled his face. The sun can kill better than the bullet, *amigo*. The trouble is she will torture you with thirst before she drains your body of life. The desert is littered with many bones.'

Bob Cooper drew in the smoke and then filtered it back through his teeth. 'Thank you, Juan Cortez. I accept your gracious offer of assistance.'

'You are a very brave man, I think.' Juan Cortez smiled at the weary hunter. 'Brave or maybe just a little crazy.'

'A man can go crazy when he's starved of company.' Bob Cooper kicked at the dust. 'Sometimes it's tough admitting that you need help.'

'A crazy man would not accept help, my friend.' Cortez snapped his fingers at the shortest and fattest of his band of men. 'Pedro, make some coffee for Cooper and myself.'

'*Si*, Juan Cortez,' the plump man nodded.

'Coffee?' Cooper raised his eyebrows as he stared at Cortez.

'We might be dusty, *amigo*, but we are civilized.' Cortez pulled out a knife from his belt and started to pick the meat from the gaps between his teeth.

FIVE

Jake Cass welcomed the morning with his usual disregard as he stood outside the old adobe. He had swilled his head under the old water pump next to the trough and now stood allowing the water to run down his worn pink underwear. He watched the trail like a man possessed by demons. They would come for his hide the moment he stopped looking for them and he never stopped looking for them. When the majority of your adult life has been dominated by killing men, women and children, the faces of your victims can haunt your every waking moment, as well as your twisted dreams. Cass had the look of a man who was haunted by those horrific memories.

'We done cooked up some bacon, Major,' Joe Watkins said as he strolled out of the smoky interior of the building. 'You wanna eat?'

'He's coming, I can hear him,' Cass said with glazed eyes.

27

'That's just the wind whistling through the saltbrush, Major Cass.' Watkins patted his boss on the back.

Cass swung around and stared at the man. 'Are you sure?'

'Yep,' Watkins nodded. 'I'm dead sure.'

Jake Cass rubbed his wet face. 'I need a shave.'

'I'll prepare some hot water for you.' Joe Watkins returned into the adobe and shook his head.

'What's wrong, Joe?' Cy Holmes asked, as he sat at the small table.

'Ain't nothing wrong,' Watkins snapped as he filled a bowl with boiling water from the small jug that rested upon the log-fuelled range.

'How far we gonna follow the major, Joe?' Holmes asked, as the older man checked the straight razor.

'To the end of the trail, Cy,' Watkins snapped.

'He ain't acting right lately Joe,' Fred Green interrupted.

Watkins glared at the two men. 'You better have the major's breakfast on this table before he finishes his shave or you boys will see how angry I can get.'

Holmes gave Green a sideways glance as the burly Watkins took the shaving gear outside. Neither man said another word about the major.

They had been riding for only a quarter of an

hour when one of Juan Cortez's riders shouted
and pointed at distant dust to their left across
the almost flat desert.

'What did he say, Cortez?' Bob Cooper asked,
as the seven riders continued through the ard
sand.

'Apache, *amigo*.' Juan Cortez shrugged.
'Miguel said that he can see Apache.'

Cooper strained his eyes but could see nothing
in the distance but shimmering images. 'Apache?
Is he sure?'

'He is very sure.' Cortez nodded, as he steered
his fine proud stallion straight ahead. 'Miguel
has the eyes of an eagle. If he says there are
Apache, then there are Apache.'

'I can't see a thing.' Cooper shook his head as
he held his reins tightly in his hands.

'They are far away and will not cause us any
trouble.' The tall Mexican stood in his stirrups
and allowed his horse to gather pace. The other
riders, including Cooper, had to spur their
mounts in order to keep up. The seven horses
reached the fertile valley and the red-roofed
hacienda within the hour. Cooper had thought
his horse a very fine specimen until he had set
eyes on the magnificent steed that Cortez rode.
It was a horse with spirit and pride that the
man from Montana truly marvelled at. He had
never seen such a creature. Bob Cooper had
ridden beside the tall Juan Cortez with the five

men following for the entire trek. It had been worth it. Cooper had not spoken at length to anyone for nearly two years and he found the Mexican an interesting and informative companion.

The group rode into the white-walled *rancho* courtyard and dismounted. Cortez stood beside Cooper as the horses were led away to the stables.

'That is sure some horseflesh,' the hunter noted.

'He is from the old country Cooper, my friend.'

'Spain?'

'Of course.' Cortez led the way into the cool building and sat down on the leather couch. The trail dust rose into the morning sunshine and drifted through the large windows, as Cooper found a seat.

'This sure is a fine place,' Cooper said, studying the room and its decoration. 'I ain't seen no finer.'

'It is OK,' Cortez said, pulling off his boots and socks. 'I would like you to rest here while I prepare for our journey.'

'Our journey?' Cooper propped his butt on the edge of the couch and watched the man. 'I ride alone, Juan Cortez.'

'Not this time.' Cortez grinned widely.

'This is my fight.' Cooper removed his Stetson and dropped it onto the small table before them.

'I can't ask anyone to help me find these men. This is my problem.'

'No need to ask for help. I shall assist you because you are seeking justice, Cooper, my friend.' Cortez reached onto the table and dragged a solid silver tray toward him. On it sat a tall crystal decanter and several glasses. 'Do you like sherry?'

'What is it?' Cooper watched as the man poured two glasses of the dark-brown liquid from the decanter.

'It is the soul of Spain. The taste of the old country.' Cortez handed one of the glasses to Cooper.

Both men drank the dark reddish-brown liquid.

'Good?'

'Pretty good.' Cooper blew out as the shock of the liquor hit his insides. 'Never tasted its like.'

Cortez stood and walked barefoot on the tiled floor. 'I am serious, *amigo*. I shall accompany you on your quest.'

Cooper slid back onto the couch still holding the glass as he watched the man holding the fine cut glass to the sunlight.

'I know this desert and you do not.'

'Juan Cortez?' Cooper said.

'Yes, *amigo*?'

'You are one heck of a strange man.'

Cortez smiled. 'Thank you, *amigo*.'

31

The Valley of Death

Bob Cooper accepted a refill and sat silently thinking as he sipped the strange liquor.

SIX

The desert heat seemed to make the mountains before the four ruthless riders appear almost like a mirage. The glare was more than their eyes could take. Only pulling their Stetsons down made riding into the brightness possible. The three riders followed the silent major as he spurred his horse at ever increasing speed toward the mountain range before them. They had always followed this man; they had never before questioned his commands, for until now he had never made a wrong move. His leadership had always been cold but militarily perfect in its simplicity, yet now, doubt had raised its ugly head in the breasts of the major's three men. Now they were not heading to some goal that they could understand such as a bank robbery or the raiding of a ranch for fresh mounts and anything else that they wished to take; now they were heading for a place that only the major seemed to know. A strange place that he had spo-

33

ken little of. A place that his three companions were beginning to wonder might simply be an aberration, the figment of a tired mind that was losing its hold on reality. Watkins, Green and Holmes still followed their leader though. Why they followed was a mystery to them all, but it had been so long now that they had grown accustomed to his leadership.

Yet since the Montana incident, they had noticed that Jake Cass grew increasingly odd in his behaviour. He talked of ghosts and things that once would never have passed his stern military lips. Watkins had always had faith in his leader, but now even he was beginning to be concerned by the man's strange behaviour and outbursts.

Yet, as with most soldiers, they seemed unable to think for themselves any longer. Orders were orders, however insane those orders might be.

Soon the four riders found a side trail at the foot of the mountains and the man with the sabre led them along it. Before they knew what was happening they found themselves on a trail that grew ever narrower as each minute ticked by. Then the trail not only grew narrower but also steeper until they were on the side of a mountain trail: to their left, a drop of unimaginable depth, whilst to their right, a sheer rock face. They followed the major on the trail like sheep trailing a ram.

The Valley of Death

Clouds of dust swirled into the air above their heads as the major led the way down off the mountain, deeper and deeper into the abyss. Unknown to any of the weary quartet, this was the place known to the local Mexicans and Indians as the Valley of Death. Only the brave or foolish ventured into its mouth for there were hidden dangers everywhere.

'Where you taking us, Major?' Watkins asked, as they rode down the slope of swirling dust. He held his reins tightly and steered his nervous horse. The dust that rose made all the mounts edgy, but his seemed even more jumpy than the others. The rough skin on his hands was starting to blister as he gripped the leather.

'We are heading to a secret place,' Cass replied over his shoulder. 'A place that few men have ever seen. A place where even the ghost will not find us, Joe.'

'But where, Major?' Watkins looked around as he clung on to his reins. The ground seemed to be crumbling beneath the horses' hooves as they descended the steep slope into the shadows. Here the sun seemed unable to penetrate although at noon it would try real hard. 'Where are we heading?'

The ex-Confederate officer gave a smiling glance back at the three followers and shook his head knowingly. The palm of his left hand rested upon the gleaming handle of his sword as he expertly urged his horse on with his reins in his right. He seemed to know where he was heading, but all three men behind him could not work out how. To their knowledge he, like themselves, had not been this far south before. So how on earth could he be leading them? All three riders watched the ever-narrowing trail beneath their horses' hooves with sweat pouring down their spines.

'Where we heading, Major?' Watkins asked his carefree leader nervously yet again. There was the sound of desperation in his normally calm voice.

'El Dorado, Joe.' Cass laughed aloud. 'We are heading to El Dorado.'

Green turned and stared at Holmes as they followed the major and Watkins down the dangerous route. Fred Green's expression said what the blond Holmes was thinking; neither rider had the courage to speak or voice their fears.

'El Dorado, Major?' Joe Watkins felt the hairs on the back of his neck start to rise in trepidation. 'Did I hear you right?'

'Yep. That's what I said.' Cass was chuckling to himself as the four men went deeper and deeper into the dark valley.

Even if Jake Cass's men had wanted to turn around and flee from this place, it would have been impossible. They had to keep going. The trail was only a mere five feet wide at its widest point and that meant they followed their leader.

They followed with a terror in their souls that their many victims must have felt over the years of carnage they had perpetrated. Now it was their turn to sweat; their turn to feel the blood freezing in their veins as they followed a man who was acting more and more irrationally.

'You serious, Major?' Watkins heard himself ask. 'Where we really headed?'

The major did not reply. He only laughed. A laugh that grew louder and louder as they rode further and further down into the darkness. It was a laugh that chilled the bones of his men. It had the sound of insanity in its resonance. Suddenly the trail widened out and they found themselves on a flat level plain between the high mountain walls.

Jake Cass raised his right arm and pulled up his reins bringing his horse to an abrupt halt.

Watkins drew his mount alongside the staring man. 'What we stop for, Major?'

'Indians,' Cass snapped, pointing ahead at the sight of a dozen or more mounted warriors sitting astride their painted ponies no more than 300 yards ahead of them on a small sand rise. The shadows from the steep cliff around them cut the scene into a contrast between dark and light.

Holmes and Green rode up beside their two companions and sat open-mouthed at the sight before them.

'Maybe they're friendly, Major,' Joe Watkins said, as the sweat started to roll down his face from under the brim of his worn Stetson. 'They might be just curious.'

'That's a war party, Joe,' Cass said through gritted teeth, as he drew his sabre and raised it above his head. 'If I'm not mistaken they are Jicarilla Apache warriors and they are pretty dangerous critters. Pretty rare to find them around here because this place is bad medicine to them.'

Watkins turned and stared at his leader. 'How can you tell what sort of Indians they are, Major? An Indian's an Indian, ain't he?'

'Before the war, these Indians raided all over Texas and New Mexico.' Jake Cass held his sabre upright so that the blade caught the sun. 'I've bumped into them before.'

'What can we do?' Cy Holmes asked nervously.

Cass laughed again and aimed his blade at the band of Indians ahead of them. 'Attack is our only hope, men.'

'Attack?' Green gasped, as he watched Cass spurring his horse forward.

'Attack,' Cass screamed as he charged toward the Apache braves. His three men drew their pistols and sank their spurs into the flesh of their horses' withers. Their animals charged after the galloping mount that carried the sword-waving major toward the motionless Apache.

The Apache suddenly realized that these were men not unlike themselves. These were not cowards who turned and ran away at the sight of their war-painted faces, these were men who raced into danger and that stunned the braves. In this canyon, retreat would have been suicidal and Cass was still soldier enough to realize this.

Screaming, the Apache kicked their ponies and rode down the sandy slope at the four approaching white renegades. Within seconds the two groups met. The knifes of the Apache were no match for the sabre that was wielded at them. The major cut his way through the Indians as if they were nothing more than hay being harvested. He chopped and hacked as his three followers used their handguns to make a route between the warriors. As the four soldiers of fortune rode up the mesa and away into the narrowing canyon beyond, they left six dead men in the dust and six wounded braves somehow still clinging to the manes of their ponies.

The Indians who still breathed rode away from the horrific scene quickly. They were headed up the long narrow trail back toward the prairie and the far-off camp where the rest of their warriors were camped. Soon, the desert would be filled with angry Apache, ready to kill anyone who crossed their path.

All that mattered to Major Jacob Cass and his blood-soaked sabre was to continue leading his

men further and further into the place known as
the Valley of Death.

SEVEN

This was no normal place that faced the four tired riders as they dismounted at the foot of the steep trail. They had been on that tortuous trail for over three hours and the sun was now at its highest point casting its light straight down into the narrow valley. Battling Apache warriors had left them stained in their enemies' dried blood. A small stream ran alongside the foot of the high walls that faced them and would serve as a means to rid themselves of the gore if not the memories. Jake Cass watched as his men brooded near their mounts with total disregard for any of them.

Only Joe Watkins had the nerve to approach his leader and ask the questions his companions were thinking. Yet even Watkins slowed to a stop when the disturbed man gazed up at him.

'What do you want Joe?' Cass spat out his words angrily at his second-in-command.

Watkins stood near the man whose eyes were

flashing around the walls of the deep canyon valley. 'Why have we come to this godforsaken place, Major?'

Cass stood like a wounded animal as he simply stared into thin air. 'Can't you see it?'

'See what?' Watkins shrugged.

'Open your eyes. Are you blind?' Cass screamed.

'See what, Major?' Casually Watkins moved closer to his superior.

Swiftly, the right hand of the major pulled his long sabre from its scabbard and pointed the keen blade at the approaching man's chest. For a brief instant both men had a mixture of fear and hatred in their eyes as they stared at one another.

Watkins hovered in his tracks and raised his arms in a gesture of surrender. The sweat ran down his face and dripped onto his vest. This was not the sweat caused by the intense heat within the valley this was fear forcing out every drop of salt from his being.

'I am not mad, Joe,' Cass screamed, as he waved the blade around. 'I am not losing my mind like you all seem to think.'

'Easy, Major, easy,' Watkins gulped. 'I know you ain't crazy but this place is—'

'El Dorado,' Cass snapped.

'What?' Watkins removed his hat and wiped the sweat off his face with his sleeve.

'Open your eyes. Open your damn' eyes.' Jake Cass raised the sabre and pointed at the rock-face before them as the sun's brilliance swooped across it.

Suddenly all three men cast their eyes where the sword of their master pointed. Then they saw the gleaming metallic ore that covered the long rocks. Its golden glow illuminated and sparkled into their weary eyes.

'Gold,' exclaimed the three men almost in unison as their leader pulled out of his breast pocket the half cigar he had been saving. Chewing on its leafy body he struck a match across the rear of his pants leg and put the flame to its tip. He grinned as he sucked on the thick smoke.

Watkins turned to face Major Jake Cass with a look of astonishment carved into his face. 'You knew about this?'

'Of course.' Cass blew a long funnel of smoke at the men as he slid his sabre back into its sheath. 'I ain't crazy, y'know. I was here a long time ago.'

A sudden wave of lost memories filled the man's face as he thought about that other life he had once led. A life that was not filled with blood and killings, not filled with constant running away from those who wanted to stretch his and his men's necks.

Holmes and Green moved beside the two men

bathed in cigar smoke. 'What is we gonna do with this gold, Major?'

Cass gave another laugh. 'We leave it where it is.'

'Leave it?' Watkins gasped.

'Yeah. You heard right,' Cass said as he moved back to his waiting horse and gathered up the loose reins. 'We leave it.'

'Why?' Cy Holmes ranted

'Yes, why, Major?' Watkins repeated his companion's question.

Cass slipped his left boot into the stirrup and hoisted himself back into the saddle. He stared down at the trio of ragged men below him and chuckled through the cigar smoke.

Fred Green rushed forward and grabbed Cass's leg. 'What do you darn well mean?'

The kick that forced Green away and onto the seat of his pants was as violent as any a mule might dish out. Jake Cass tossed away his cigar and reined his horse tightly. 'Fools. Fools.'

Joe Watkins helped Green back onto his feet as he watched their leader stand in his stirrups.

'This ain't nothing,' Cass shouted at his men. 'This is just the tip of the iceberg.'

'What ya mean, Major?' Holmes shrugged.

Cass pointed down the long flat trail that led between the tall mountain walls. 'That's where we gotta go. Down there is the real treasure, just waiting for us to take.'

All three men mounted their horses and drew alongside the major.

'Follow me, boys.' Jake Cass spurred his horse masterfully and led the way through the narrow canyon. Suddenly he appeared to have the energy that had been lacking over recent days. Now he seemed almost back to his former self. His men followed as they had always followed. Wherever they were going they were going fast. The sound of their thundering hooves echoed around the high walls that were laced with gold. Whether or not the strange major had redeemed himself in the eyes of his dwindling army, was another thing.

This was indeed a lonely place, yet the four renegade soldiers had not been alone since they had left the relative safety of the old deserted adobe earlier that morning. The arid scenery hid many things from the riders as they made their way along the dry canyon floor through the desolate valley. Eyes had been watching the four invaders' every move. Eyes that saw all and yet were never seen. Eyes that belonged to one of the many people who dwelled in this stark vast land.

This was indeed the Valley of Death and those who lived here were experts at survival against the most severe odds that nature could muster against them. This place had earned its name not just because of its tortuous landscapes of 5,000 feet tall mesas and its valleys that seemed carved out of solid rock by God Himself, as he made a trail that headed straight into the jaws of Hell, but because of the people who ruled this land. They had lived in this unholy place for longer than the white man had been in America, and who guarded this place for its spirituality. They were its keepers.

The eyes continued to plot the four riders' every move through the network of canyons trimmed with golden ledges. The eyes belonged to the strange and ancient ones: the people known simply as the Seri.

Major Cass and his three men did not know it yet but soon they would find out that the Seri did not tolerate strangers or invaders lightly.

They were the brothers of the snake. They were the keepers of the secret that many had sought. All who entered the Valley of Death soon realized why it had this name. The Seri took no prisoners. Only one white man had managed to escape this place and that man was Major Jake Cass.

EIGHT

Bob Cooper sat outside the stables in the court-yard of his newly found protector Juan Cortez wondering why this total stranger seemed so interested in him and his fate. Answers seemed to evade him. The man could not understand how anyone would wish to help him and his very singular purpose.

It was now early evening and the sun was going through its slow regular process of sinking into the desert beyond the large ranch. The heat was quickly evaporating in the impressive court-yard. Cooper had stayed awake for little more than fifteen minutes after taking advantage of the kind offer of a real bed shortly after their arrival. He had slept his usual sleep that did lit-tle to aid his rest. The constant images invading his dreams, turning them into nightmares, still haunted the lone hunter. Even the soft duck-down mattress had not soothed his torment and heartache.

His eyes still caked in trail dust caught sight of a figure moving from one small building to another, lighting hanging lanterns as she went. Resting his chin on his knuckles, he sat watching the slim female with an interest that he had long thought gone. She had hair that reached down to the base of her spine. Black shining hair that seemed to flow as she moved with a grace that he had not witnessed for many years. As this young woman moved around the area with her burning taper cupped in her small hands, she kept casting her large black eyes in his direction. Cooper watched her and found himself smiling as she drew close to him. She pulled a small chain that lowered the lantern outside the stables and lit the wick inside the glass case. She pushed the lantern back up into its regular position and then stood facing the tired man. The light from the taper in her hands gave Bob Cooper a clear view of her attractive face.

'You are Cooper?' she asked with lips that blew out the flickering taper.

'Yes, ma'am. I'm Cooper.' He smiled, feeling guilty for being so dirty in the presence of what clearly was a lady.

'My brother spoke of you.'

'Juan Cortez is your brother?'

'*Si*. I am Rosa.' Her eyes seemed to flutter as she spoke to the tired man. 'My brother say you are seeking evil men and he is going to help you.'

'Your brother is a mighty generous man, Rosa.' Cooper felt a sudden rush of blood as she stepped cautiously closer to him.

'Juan is a fool but he is a good man.' She moved gracefully before him, her breasts heaving inside the small, tight, low-cut top.

Cooper found himself staring at the small golden crucifix that rested between her softly tanned bosom. 'He wants to fight my battles for me, I guess.'

'He might wish to fight for you because he can see you are exhausted, Cooper.' Rosa Cortez moved even closer to him. Now her natural perfume filled his nostrils reaching a place that had not been reached for many years.

'How old are you Rosa?'

'Oh, I am very old Cooper.' Her face glowed as she spoke and hinted of pleasures he had forgotten existed. 'I am nearly eighteen years old.'

'That is old,' he grinned. 'I am twice that age.'

'But it is good for a man to be old.' Rosa touched his hair as if searching for white hairs. There were none. 'For a woman to be over sixteen and not betrothed is very sad.'

'I think you've still got a little time left.'

Suddenly the sound of a door opening and closing across the courtyard now bathed in moon and lamplight, caught both their attentions. Rosa gave Cooper a small peck on the cheek.

'I see you again.'

Cooper watched as she hurried away into a building directly opposite the stables. His fingers touched his unshaven cheek where her soft lips had kissed him.

The tall figure of Juan Cortez left the main building with the short Pedro at his side and headed directly towards him. Cooper rose to his feet and ran his hand through his hair. Although his eyes were watching the two approaching men, his thoughts were upon the beautiful girl who had just departed his company.

'My friend is rested?' Cortez asked placing a hand upon Cooper's shoulder.

'Yep,' Cooper answered. 'I had a sleep after that meal your servants prepared me.'

Cortez raised an eyebrow. 'You did not sleep the sleep of angels, Cooper.'

'What you getting at?'

'Your sleep was troubled.' Cortez waved for the fat Pedro to leave them; the man obeyed. 'I hear you from downstairs.'

'I ain't used to soft beds.' Cooper tried to disguise his problems. 'Sorry.'

Cortez rested a foot upon the edge of the bench. 'I think you are a very sad man.'

'So?' Cooper sighed as his eyes kept drifting across to the building that Rosa had entered, as if wanting to catch another glimpse of the fascinating female.

'I was once the same, *amigo*,' Cortez confessed

to the stranger. 'You are haunted by past events. You are haunted by the thoughts that drive you on this dangerous quest.'

'I can't help remembering things, can I?' Cooper seemed angry.

'True. Yet sometimes we, the living, prevent our dear departed from finding true peace in Heaven.' Cortez pulled out two of his long cigars and forced one into Cooper's hand. 'We must learn to move on. They must rest in peace.'

Cooper accepted the light and drew in the smoke. 'How can you ask me to forget my wife and child?'

'Never forget, but do not try to remember.' Cortez gazed at the moon above his ranch with an awe in his face that was almost childlike. 'Let them rest.'

'I understand what you're saying.' Cooper blew out the strong smoke and moved alongside the tall Mexican.

'Did I see Rosa with you when I came out from the *hacienda*, Cooper?' Juan Cortez rolled his cigar around in his lips as if cooling it with his saliva.

'You did.' Cooper watched the ground as they spoke.

'You like my little sister?'

Cooper paused and looked up into the face of his host. 'She is a very nice young woman.'

'Very big for her age too.' Juan Cortez smiled.

51

'Not so big for someone nearly eighteen.'

Cortez laughed. 'She is sixteen, but old enough.'

'Sixteen?' Cooper pulled hard on the cigar. He was twenty years older than Rosa and yet it did not seem to matter.

An hour later they had finished an entire decanter of sherry and another two cigars. The talk had centred upon whether or not Juan Cortez would accompany Cooper after the four renegades who had fled into the Valley of Death. Neither man would be budged from his position; Cortez insisted on going with Cooper and Cooper was adamant that he would continue alone. During the evening meal they still pressed their points and insisted that they were both correct. During the long meal, Rosa had sat silently eating and listening to both men's points of view. She said nothing because she felt the two men were correct and yet both completely wrong. How could she take sides?

After the meal was finished, the two men continued their good-humoured argument back into the large room. Neither man wished the other to go on this trek because they knew it would involve a showdown which might cost their lives. It was as if neither man could face the prospect of the other being killed by the renegades.

'Stalemate,' Rosa said, walking across the tiled living-room floor toward the two seated men.

'Pardon, my little sister?' Juan Cortez turned his head at the sound of his bare-footed sister's voice.

As she placed the tray down on the low table, she knelt and lifted the engraved silver coffee pot and poured three cups of the black brew. 'I said, stalemate, Juan.'

'Yes, but what do you mean, Rosa?' Cortez leaned forward on the couch.

'I have listened to you both for many hours and I am getting very bored.' She flashed her eyes briefly at Cooper making him suddenly sit upright in his chair. 'Stalemate is what you say in chess when there is no winner, is it not?'

Juan Cortez turned to Cooper and shrugged. 'Stalemate, *amigo*.'

NINE

NINE

It seemed like looking up a thousand miles from the floor of the canyon to the stars in the dark sky. The moon was hidden from view by the tall rock walls that seemed to lean into one another from either side of the narrow valley. The campfire worked hard to illuminate the tall walls around the four men. It had been an hour since the major had called a halt to their trek and decided this was as good a place to camp as any. They had unsaddled their horses and laid out their bedrolls around the fire made of brush and dry kindling. Their saddles were to be their pillows for the thousandth time since they had struck out together on the road to theft and butchery. They had shared out the jerky and their last two cans of pork and beans as they waited for the coffee grounds to boil up in the black pot they had sat in the centre of the flames. Cy Holmes chewed on jerky whilst listening to the older men's dull conversation.

The Valley of Death

Major Jake Cass sat with his campaign coat wrapped around him watching the flames licking the black coffee pot. Joe Watkins rested against his saddle trying to sleep but unable in this strange overwhelming place and Fred Green kept adding twigs to the fire.

This was not how the major remembered this place all those years ago when he still had his youth. This place seemed more evil than then. Thoughts kept invading his mind as he watched the never ceasing flames licking the air between them. Thoughts of the last time he had entered this place. Thoughts that were more like a dream than reality. Had it truly been reality? The old soldier chewed on his last chunk of jerky and watched his men before him. It had come down to this, he thought. Three men out of an entire army troop. Where had they all gone since the surrender? He forced back the memory of all his dead men and refused to allow their images to fill his brain with their young trusting faces. He had started out right. He had been decorated by Lee himself for valour. How had it all turned out like this? Where did the honour go and be replaced with the killing and the raping and the stealing? What had happened?

Could it ever end? He shook his head as he gazed about his last three men. Were they always as evil as now? Had it been the war that had turned them into what they now were? So

many questions that could never be answered.
Then he tried to remember the last time he had
been into this cold chilling place and knew there
was something he had forgotten; some reason
why this place remained untouched by the white
man unlike other places. He knew that his mind
no longer functioned the way it once had and
that worried him. He had blocked out so many
things that he could no longer face or admit to,
so many things that he had done, he had ordered
to be done and watched being done. This place
brought back the shadows that he tried to dis-
miss from his soul.

This place had once almost taken his young
life and he thought back to how it had been. He
gazed about the orange-gold walls of the rockface
about their small campsite and tried to recall
what had once happened. It was now just a blur.

Just a blur that he could not or would not
bring back into focus so that he could see what
was disturbing him so. Major Jacob Harvey Cass
sat with his three men feeling alone, very much
alone without even his memories to comfort him.

It was the younger Cy Holmes who first
noticed something up on the rocks. It was something out of the ordinary in the rocks that
seemed to reach up at the stars. He screwed up
his eyes trying to get a better look at whatever it
was that had caught his attention, but it had
gone. He felt the sweat trickling slowly down his

back under his shirt and overcoat. He used his index finger to poke up his Stetson off his brow and tried to focus his eyes at the flickering shadowy images before him.

'What's wrong, Cy?' Fred Green asked the blond man, as he dropped twig after twig onto the fire before him.

Cy Holmes blew out a sigh of condensed fear. 'Did you see that, Fred?'

'There ain't nothing to see, Cy,' Green laughed. 'You're getting spooked by the shadows, that's all. Take it easy.'

'Did you see it, Major?' Holmes said quietly across the camp-fire to his leader.

Cass looked up at the blond man whose words brought him back to this strange place. 'What?'

'Did you see that?' Holmes pointed up at the rocks that seemed to glow in the light of the fire. 'I seen something moving up there.'

'You're just worn out, Cy,' Green said, dropping even more kindling onto the fire. 'Get some shut eye.'

Holmes crawled around the hot camp-fire and sat next to the motionless figure of the major. 'I saw a figure up there, Major. I did see someone. Honest.'

Jake Cass's eyes drifted onto the face of the youngest of his men. He studied the face for several moments before believing him. 'Was it the hunter?'

Cy Holmes shook his head. 'It moved too fast for a white man.'

Cass tipped his Stetson up off his face and gazed around the massive rock face that shimmered in the light of their fire. His steady eyes moved around the endless area before he, too, thought he saw something. 'I guess you're right, Cy.'

'Who are they Major?' Holmes asked, fear in his voice.

'Indians, boy,' Cass sighed.

'Apache?'

Jake Cass stared at Cy Holmes again. 'Not Apache.'

'Then what tribe are they?' Holmes looked like a raccoon up a tree staring down at a mess of hounds.

'Ain't sure.' Cass rubbed his chin. 'I recall that they are a secret tribe that have a strange religion. They ain't Apache though.'

'I don't like this, Major,' Cy Holmes sniffled. 'We are like apples in a barrel here. Sitting ducks.'

'Get the carbines out of the saddle skins,' Cass commanded, leaning over and shaking Watkins.

Joe Watkins lifted his hat and stared into the face of the major. 'What's the matter?'

'We got company, Joe,' Cass informed him. 'Get up and keep your eyes open.'

Watkins sat upright as Holmes passed the

Winchesters around to his companions. Watkins cocked his rifle and then started to search the rocks for targets with his sleepy eyes. He could not see anything but trusted his commanding officer's judgement.

'We don't open up unless they attack, boys,' Cass ordered.

'Suits me,' Holmes gulped.

'How can you shoot something you can't see?' Watkins sat nervously holding his rifle across his middle. 'Who are they Major?'

'Indians,' Cass replied.

'I ain't 'feared of no damn Indians, Major.' Watkins gave a belly laugh.

Major Cass glared at his second-in-command. 'Fear these Indians, Joe. They are different.'

Watkins's face suddenly lost the smile that had been covering it and he felt the words spoken by his leader. 'They got carbines, Major?'

'They don't need carbines,' Cass mumbled. 'But we sure do.'

Only Green seemed uninterested. He either did not believe his companions or he was simply too exhausted to care.

'That coffee ready, Fred?' Cass asked, sliding bullets into his Winchester.

'Yep, Major,' Green replied.

'Then pour us some,' Cass ordered.

'Sure thing, Major.' Green lifted the heavy coffee pot up off the flames using his bandanna as

protection against the heat and poured out a cup
for the major. 'Pass this to the—'

Fred Green did not have time to finish his sen-
tence. Falling forward into the flames, the pot
still clutched in his dead hand, he was gone.
Holmes reached into the fire and pulled out his
friend's burning body and rolled it into the sand.
Then his young eyes saw it. An arrow. The arrow
had entered the back of Green's neck and forced
its way through; the point dripped with blood
over the young man who held the lifeless body.

'Fred! Fred!' Holmes screamed at the lifeless
body that still smouldered in his arms.

'He's a goner, boy,' Watkins shouted at the
youngster. 'Watch your back or you'll be joining
him pretty damn quick.'

Holmes watched as Watkins dragged his saddle around and lay behind it trying to become as
small a target as possible, clutching his carbine
tightly. Cy Holmes finally dropped his dead
friend and picked up his Winchester once more
and copied Watkins's action.

Only Major Cass remained sitting against his
saddle holding his rifle by the fire still sliding
bullets into its side chamber as if nothing had
happened. He was nodding to himself as he suddenly remembered the last time he had entered
the Valley of Death with another handful of men.
On that occasion he was the youngest and as fate
would have it, the luckiest. For he alone had

managed to escape. It all came flooding back to him and he knew who the enemy were and in how dangerous a spot he had placed them.

'Take cover, Major. Goddamnit,' Watkins yelled.

Cass glanced down at his remaining two men and smiled. 'Watch your language, Joe. Officer on parade.'

'Take cover, Major.' Holmes repeated his friend's words to the calm officer. 'Please take cover.'

'The Indians are gonna get you for sure,' Watkins raged.

'They are the Seri.' Cass smiled down at his men. 'They do not take prisoners.'

'Major. Take cover.'

'There ain't much point, boys,' Cass sighed. 'Ain't much point at all.'

TEN

Bob Cooper had attempted to rise earlier than his host, Juan Cortez, and get out of the ranch alone. However much he liked the Mexican, he felt that it was not worth risking two lives in his mission to catch up with Cass and company. Cooper had dressed and gathered up his saddlebags with their few contents and left his room. Dawn had only just broken according to the rooster out on the roof of the henhouse, but Cooper moved effortlessly. He walked down the tiled stone staircase with its cast-iron banister into the spacious living-room just as the first rays of the morning sun came sneaking through the glass of the wide windows. He moved quietly across the massive room so as not to disturb any of the household and servants and opened the door leading to the courtyard. Out in the fresh morning air he took a refreshing drink from the barrel perched on the wall of the well before heading toward the stables. It was a long walk past smaller buildings that functioned like a well-oiled machine to keep the ranch completely independent of the outside world. As Cooper calmly entered the dark place filled with impressive animals he rested the saddle-bags on the ground before moving to the neck of his horse, making soothing noises as he went. He stroked the animal's neck as he saw its large right eye focus on him.

'You are not leaving, *amigo*?'

Cooper swung around and searched for the recognizable voice that had shaken him. 'Juan Cortez.'

Juan Cortez rose to his feet from the comfort of the bale of hay he had used as a bed and smiled at the man. 'I knew you were not the sort of man to allow the charity of assistance to help you.'

'What?' Cooper moved out of the shadows to face the taller man. 'What did you say?'

'I do not know.' Cortez smiled broadly. 'I do not listen to myself talking.'

The two men squared up to each other before looking up and down as if inspecting the other's condition. There was humour in both their faces. The tall Mexican had a disarming way of smiling that Cooper had never seen in any other person. It intrigued the hunter.

'You must not leave just yet, *amigo*.' Cortez put his arm around the shoulder of Cooper.

'You can't force me to stay,' Cooper shrugged.

'I can force you to have breakfast.' The taller man grinned with all his charm.

'I gotta go,' Cooper fumed. 'The trail will go cold. I might never catch up to those bastards.'

'I know where they are.' Cortez gave a hearty laugh. 'I had Miguel and Pedro go out yesterday to seek them out for us.'

'Us?'

'For you, Cooper. For you.' Juan Cortez started to move back toward his house with his arm pulling Bob Cooper with him. 'There is no hurry.'

'So your men have located them?' Bob Cooper felt the blood surge into his neck muscles as he thought about the renegades.

'*Si, amigo.*' Cortez stopped when Cooper refused to move any further toward the white-washed building. 'My men have told me exactly where they are. Believe me, we have all the time in the world.'

'Where are they, Juan Cortez?' Cooper stared hard at the tall man. 'Just tell me where those varmints are and I'll be out of here.'

Cortez grinned. 'I cannot explain. But I can show you easily if you will allow?'

Cooper knew that it was no longer worth arguing with his host and started to laugh. It was a laughter of mixed emotion. A laughter that had to admit he was being outwitted every inch of the way by the tall lean Latin American.

'You ever lose an argument?' Cooper sighed.

'We are both winners, Cooper.' Cortez patted the shorter man on his back. 'You require my expertise. It is yours because I understand what drives you on this crusade.'

'You talk real fancy.'

'Do you know that my little sister Rosa is very beautiful in the morning?' Juan Cortez leaned down to look into his friend's face. 'So very beautiful, Cooper, my friend.'

'What's that got to do with me?'

'That depends upon Rosa.'

Bob Cooper started to aim his boots at the house once more as the smell of cooking filled his nostrils. 'Can we head out after breakfast, Cortez?'

'Call me Juan,' Cortez laughed. 'We shall be like brothers riding out into the prairie. Our pistols loaded and our bellies pretty filled too.'

'Is that yes, Juan?'

Bob Cooper hesitated as they approached the doorway into the elegant house. Rosa stood in the frame smiling at him. A smile that no man could resist. The hunter felt the firm hand of his tall friend in the middle of his back pushing him forward toward the incredibly gorgeous female.

'Cooper,' she sighed, staring at him with eyes that seemed to melt into his soul.

'Rosa,' Cooper somehow replied.

The Valley of Death

Bob Cooper soon discovered that Juan Cortez was truly a man of his word, who went far beyond his promises for reasons that he kept secreted deep within himself. He himself led out the two horses from the stables across the wide courtyard up to the large whitewashed *hacienda*. When he reached the hitching rail he released the reins and allowed the two beasts to drink from the trough as he checked the girths.

Pedro Ramera followed his employer the way a dog trails its master. He hovered around the tall Cortez watching everything the man did as if waiting for instructions. None came. Cortez pulled up his large black sombrero from where it had rested upon his back and placed it onto his head. He looked every inch the ruler of a mythical land. Like his Spanish forbears he had cool blood racing through his veins.

'Why cannot we go with you and the *gringo*, Juan Cortez?' the short rotund man asked. 'We will protect you from the evil ones whom he seeks.'

'Am I a coward, Pedro?' Cortez smiled down at the man. 'Do I require his mother's breast to nurse him?'

'They are bad men.' Pedro shook his head as he crossed himself. 'You cannot face such vermin without your men at your side.'

'I am Juan Cortez,' the tall man informed him. 'I need no army to help a friend.'

'This *gringo* is not your friend; he is a stranger.'

Cortez raised a finger that silenced the fat man. 'Go away and do not question me any more.'

Pedro bowed and hurried away.

Cortez stood proudly beside his noble stallion as he watched his men around the courtyard. He knew that they all felt the same as Pedro but he felt that he was right. He knew that if he snapped his fingers they would all saddle up and join him on this quest for justice. One snap of his fingers. He pulled out a cigar from his inside breast pocket and bit off its tip before placing it between his white teeth. The match ignited as he ran it along the wall of the big house and he casually put the flame to the cigar. As he sucked in the smoke he looked through his black eyebrows at his men once more before turning and entering the building.

'Are you ready, *amigo*?'

Bob Cooper looked up from the long leather couch where he waited beside the beautiful Rosa. 'Yeah. I'm ready.'

Cortez watched as the troubled man got to his feet and adjusted his gunbelt. Rosa stood up next to him, her lips silent as she watched the man pulling on his coat and picking his Stetson up off the low table. Cooper glanced at her momentarily as he placed his hat over his hair.

Both men stared into each other's eyes and

saw each other's scared souls. Neither could make eye contact with the beautiful female beside them.

Each felt love for this young woman, but love that was different to both of them.

'I gotta go, Rosa,' Bob Cooper heard himself mutter as he dragged himself away from her. She did not touch him with her fingers or her hands but she touched him all the same. Cooper felt as if he were breaking free from a hidden force that had melted them together during their brief encounter. For the first time in two years he suddenly felt like a man who might just have a future, but one that depended upon his burying the past.

She followed the two men out into the early morning sunshine silently. Respectfully. She was young, very young, but she knew what she wanted and he was getting onto a horse next to her older brother. Her eyes watched the man named Cooper as he sat in his saddle and pulled out his Winchester to check it before sliding it back into its sheath.

'We have plenty of water.' Cortez pointed to the three canteens hanging from both their saddlehorns. 'Water is the most valuable item out there, my friend.'

'That I know from experience, Juan.' Cooper pulled his reins tight in his hands as he sat watching the girl below him. She looked the way a female ought to look, he thought.

The Valley of Death

Juan Cortez turned his black pure-bred stallion away from the *hacienda*. 'Do not worry yourself, little sister.'

Rosa remained silent as she simply watched them.

Cooper hauled his horse away from the hitching rail and sank his spurs into the horse's quarters. The two men rode out into the fertile land that surrounded the ranch and were soon galloping across ground that became increasingly dry and more arid with every hoofbeat.

Cooper had deliberately not looked into Rosa Cortez's eyes before leaving the courtyard of the ranch. He knew that if he had done so, he would have seen the one thing that would have ended his quest. He would have witnessed the tears of a good woman who felt for him the way that he felt for her.

ELEVEN

The Valley of Death was its name, the mysterious tribe called the Seri, its faithful guardians. The sun had been creeping higher and higher over the towering mountains that surrounded the narrow canyon where Major Jake Cass had waited for several hours now. Unlike Watkins and Holmes who had lain nervously upon their bellies all night waiting for the attack that had not come he had dozed against his saddle quite happily.

Fred Green's body still lay across the ashes where it had been slain by the Seri arrow. Flies started to gather as they sensed the body rotting in the normally sterile sand, their noise growing louder with every passing second as the heat grew on the canyon floor.

As he woke, Cass smiled at his two remaining men. 'Still alive?'

Watkins crawled beside his leader with an expression upon his sleep-starved face that echoed all the horrors an awakening nightmare had to offer. 'What is going on, Major?'

'We're alive, Joe.' Jake Cass stood and brushed the dust from his pants before picking up his sabre and clipping it to his belt. 'And this place is starting to stink real bad.'

'Why didn't they attack?' Watkins rose up and faced the calm man. 'Why did they slaughter Fred and then do nothing to harm the rest of us, Major?'

The Major rubbed the sweat off his brow as his cold eyes burned into the youngster.

'They killed Fred as a warning. Now we are supposed to retreat with our damn tails between our legs.'

'Well, Major?' Holmes asked fearfully.

'Bury Fred's body,' Cass said. 'I ain't gonna start retreating now.'

Cy Holmes nodded and did as he was ordered. Using his hands as shovels, he dug a shallow grave in the soft sand before rolling Fred Green's twisted body into it. Then he pushed the white sand over the horrible sight.

Joe Watkins fought against his burning eyes that begged to close and find slumber as he watched the two men before him; one confused and pitiful whilst the other strangely angry.

'Saddle the horses.' Jake Cass pointed at Watkins. 'We go on.'

'Go on?' Watkins staggered toward the man in the grey hat.

'Exactly.'

'In God's name why? Why?' Watkins watched the figure of his superior wander around the ashes of the camp-fire.

'To get out of here, man,' Cass snapped.

'But why not return along the trail that we came down?'

'That is what they want us to do,' Cass snorted. 'I know these people and how they think. We have to go on. It's our only chance. Besides, those Indians will probably be waiting for us at the entrance to the valley.'

'But, Major. . ?'

'We have only one chance. Stick with me and we'll be leaving this hell-hole rich men.' Cass nodded without any emotion upon his face.

Holmes picked up his saddle and moved toward his horse slowly without looking at either of his companions. All his eyes could focus upon were the mountainous rocks above them, unlike the solid-framed figure of Watkins who blew out a huge sigh of exhaustion before hoisting up his own saddle off the soft ground. Without another word of complaint to Cass, he moved alongside his mount and tossed the blanket over the creature's wide back before hauling the saddle on top of it. Cass was pacing and muttering to himself as his men worked at following his orders.

'I beat these devils once and I can do it again, men,' Cass said, as he walked around the ashes of the previous evening's camp-fire. Suddenly, Watkins and Holmes gasped as their once great leader Jacob Cass stooped and drew his Winchester from its leather sheath beside his saddle and swung around to face them with a look in his eyes that they had seen many times over the past few years. As fast as he had gathered up his carbine he lifted it at the mountainside and fired a single shot.

To their horror and surprise they heard a scream echoing above their heads. Turning, they watched as a strangely adorned Indian fell into the canyon. A cloud of dust rose around the broken body as Cass walked toward the corpse. Then Cass swung around, cocked his Winchester and fired again. This time the sound of his bullet bouncing off the rocks above echoed around the canyon as an arrow landed between his legs. Cass primed his carbine again and fired another shot that found its mark. Glancing across at his stunned men he motioned with the long barrel for them to get their rifles. Both men did so, feverishly trying to see their enemy. It seemed to both Holmes and Watkins that only the major had eyes that could find these creatures.

Never lowering his rifle he stood above the broken body and sighed to himself.

His two men moved quickly to Cass's side with their primed rifles aiming up at the glittering rock face.

Cass kicked the Indian's body several times before he started talking to his men. 'See this critter?'

Watkins gazed down at the dead man. He was smaller than any Indian they had ever encountered previously on their travels and was covered in white paint. He wore a strange headdress that also was unlike anything they had ever seen before. It was small and shaped like an upside-down bird's nest and it too was covered in a chalky substance.

'This, gentlemen, is a Seri,' Cass informed them.

'Why is he painted up like that, Major?' Watkins asked, as he tried to keep his attention on the rocks above them. He feared ending up like Green with a well-placed arrow in his throat.

'I told you about ghosts, didn't I?' Cass gritted his teeth when he talked as if remembering things any normal man would try to blot from his memory.

'Ghosts?' Young Cy Holmes was shaking as he stared at the white body at the major's feet.

'They are known as the Snake people, men.' Cass cocked his rifle again.

'Snake people?' Cy Holmes gulped once more, trying not to shake as much as his voice did.

Jake Cass sneered at the sight of the Indian beside his boots. 'Snake people.'

Cass pushed his men back toward the horses. 'Saddle my mount. Use Fred's horse as a pack animal.'

As the two tired and fearful men saddled the horses they wondered if a man could cheat the Devil twice in one lifetime.

TWELVE

The two riders had made exceptionally good progress across the wide desert that consisted of tall cactus and varied clumps of sagebrush and saltbrush embedded in white sand that was so devilishly hot during the noon sun, that no living creature could stand motionless upon it for very long without receiving severe burns. Hot, white, burning sand. This was a place where all living creatures sought shadows. They meant the difference between life and death in this tortuous inferno. Directly overhead, the blazing sun beat down unmercifully upon them as they headed toward the distant mesa. It was hard to see anything clearly as the desert started to play its usual games. The haze wove a shimmering image before their advancing horses but this did not slow their progress.

Bob Cooper had given his mount full rein as it galloped just slightly behind the stallion under Juan Cortez. The Mexican held his noble animal back as they rode, knowing that Cooper's horse could never keep up the pace of which his mount was capable.

Hour upon hour they had ridden only stopping to water their horses and themselves periodically. This was no normal afternoon ride in the countryside, this was a battle with the elements and both riders knew that the odds were stacked heavily against them.

They rode and rode as if possessed by demons that would not allow them to stop. Cortez was neither foolhardy nor a man used to taking needless risks yet he knew the pain that filled his companion's heart only too well. He had suffered a similar devastation himself years earlier. This was a subject he never discussed but never ever forgot. Riding with Cooper was no mere whim, this was an act of compassion. Vengeance was one thing he understood only too well. He had lived as Cooper lived with nothing but revenge in his soul until one day he realized that revenge was not destroying his enemies, only himself. Seeing Bob Cooper with eyes that not only had sight but vision, he vowed to stick with this lone hunter. Secretly, he felt that Cooper might have ridden too far down that soul-destroying road and be unable to turn back.

He led the way to the place that his men had instructed him was where they would locate the fleeing renegades. Cooper followed but knew little of their destination. All he cared about was finding the men who had ruined his life so many long months previously. If the tall Mexican had ventured the information that they were headed for the Valley of Death, it would have meant nothing to him.

Only those born in this desolate desert knew of the forbidden places. The Valley of Death had many legends associated with it and some were simply that, whilst other stories had a basis in hard fact.

There were stories that an ancient ghost tribe of Indians dwelled in the mountains and canyons that made up the entire range of the mesa. A tribe that was thought to have long since died out in other places; one that even the Apache would not face. Legends filled the minds of imaginative people as well as those who were simply stupid.

Cortez reined in his stallion hard and stood in his stirrups as the horse stopped in its tracks. The clouds of dust that rose above their heads as Cooper also pulled up his horse swiried about them in the hot dry air. It was several minutes before they could once again see the area before them.

'Why did we stop, Juan?' Cooper raised his sore butt off the saddle and allowed the air to circulate beneath his jeans.

Cortez sat upright in his saddle and glanced across at his new-found friend. 'See it?'

Bob Cooper could tell by the tone in Cortez's voice that he was serious. 'See what exactly?'

Cortez pointed a long finger at the clouds of dust rising directly ahead of them. Cooper lifted a hand to shield his stare from the blindingly hot sun. It took a while before he was able to focus against the heat-haze.

'Mirage?' he queried, looking back at the Mexican who was lighting another of his long cigars. 'Ain't that a mirage?'

'I think not, Cooper, my friend.' Cortez pulled the smoke from his mouth. 'That is horses. A lot of horses.'

'Horses?' Cooper grinned. 'Wild horses?'

'That is not a herd of mustangs.' Juan Cortez sucked hard on the brown smoke. 'That is Indians, I think.'

'Apache?' Cooper had a dread of Apache after hearing so many tales of their exploits.

'I think so.'

'Where they headed?'

'Straight at us, I think.' Cortez flicked the ash off the cigar and then drew his mount closer to his companion. He looked long and hard with eyes more used to this climate than the lone hunter's. The dust was between them and the far-off mesa where he knew the entrance to the Valley of Death lay. He offered his cigar to Cooper who accepted it and took one drag before returning it. 'They have seen our dust.'

'Are they coming to fight?' Cooper felt a chill even though the heat of the powerful sun burned into his body.

'They are coming to kill.' Cortez raised his eyebrows and tried to look indifferent. 'This is their place; we are intruders.'

'What we gonna do?' Bob Cooper asked, as the smoke drifted out between his teeth.

'That is a very good question, *amigo*.' Cortez pulled his sombrero down over his eyes and then tossed the half-used cigar away. 'Apache can be most aggressive.'

'We able to ride around them?' Cooper felt edgy as he sat holding onto his reins. For the first time in two years he felt the sense of fear riding into his soul.

Cortez surveyed the horizon carefully until he was satisfied that he had a reasonable plan. He pointed to their left where the cactus were as tall as trees.

'What's over that way, Juan?' Cooper wiped his fare with his bandanna.

'A detour.' Cortez patted his friend's back as he shook his reins and jabbed his spurs. 'And a lot of sand.'

The two riders galloped east hard leaving a wake of dust rising behind them. Pulling up briefly, both men looked at the clouds of dust to their right. The Indians were coming at them hard and fast. So far neither the Apache nor

Cooper and Cortez had caught sight of each other. All any of them could see was each other's dust floating thick on the ground and high above the desert.

Then the two riders heard the sound of rifles firing behind them and felt the bullets whizzing past their heads.

'Keep riding, *amigo*,' Cortez screamed over the noise of further rifle shots.

Bob Cooper kept his head down and rode as hard as he knew how beside the expert horseman.

Cortez signalled with his head that they change direction and both riders burst off through the tall cactus-littered dunes that were dotted along a sleepy draw. Cooper rode as if his horse's tail was about to catch fire and stayed just behind the proud, bolting stallion. With the speed that the thoroughbred stallion was capable of he knew that if Juan Cortez had wanted, he could have left him behind, being chased by the Apache war party. Yet Cortez was holding back his horse so that the hunter could keep up.

It seemed that they were now heading at the rising dust-clouds that they wished to avoid. They were. The Mexican had a plan that beggared belief.

Once more they stopped. This time Juan Cortez pulled his rope off his saddlehorn and tossed it over a tall cactus.

The Valley of Death

'You do the same, *amigo*,' he cried to Cooper as the sound of the approaching Apache grew louder and louder in both men's ears.

Bob Cooper did as he was told and lassoed a huge cactus before wrapping the remainder of his rope around his saddlehorn.

'Now what, Juan?' he asked as the noise of whooping Indians filled the air above the draw.

Cortez spurred his stallion and started dragging the cactus behind his horse. 'Do this.'

Cooper spurred his horse hard and chased after the Mexican with his cactus in tow. He drew level with the laughing man just as a wall of half-naked Apache warriors spilled over the top of the dunes and down into the draw.

'Ride, *amigo*. Ride like you never rode before.'

Cooper had no problem with that suggestion as he could almost feel the hot screaming breath of the braves on his neck. Both riders rode hard dragging the cactus, sending clouds of dust billowing behind them. Faster and faster they rode, side by side. The two men rode in a full circle across the churned-up ground of sagebrush, leaving more and more swirling dust-clouds in their wake. They knew that they had the war party confused as to which direction to aim their ponies and that was their intention.

Cooper stuck alongside Juan Cortez as they rode. When Cortez turned to the right, so did he. When the Mexican dragged his stallion to the left, Cooper stayed right there with him. Soon the dust was so thick that the Indians could be heard but no longer seen. Faster and faster Cortez displayed his superior knowledge of this dry lifeless place to the newcomer alongside him. Then when the dust was at its densest, Cortez freed his rope and dropped it before spurring his mount to take flight. It was only a matter of seconds before Bob Cooper found himself copying the true master. Both riders rode up a dune and straight down the other side before galloping at breakneck speed down toward the Valley of Death. Without pausing, Cortez broke every taboo in this area and hurtled down into the narrow trail followed closely by the hunter.

The Apache had been right on their heels as they charged through the dense dust-clouds. They could almost touch the two riders ahead of them and yet the braves covered in war paint had reined up and stopped their pursuit. The Apache watched as the two men disappeared into the dark lonely trail. The dust that rose from their horses' hooves seemed to swallow them whole in the minds of the superstitious war party.

Cooper and Cortez had heard the Indians after them but then the sound of the warriors ceased. The tall Mexican knew why the braves had ended their chase even if Bob Cooper did not.

The Valley of Death

The two riders continued for several minutes descending down the dark shadow-covered trail before slowing up their horses to a steady trot. They were on the narrow trail that led down into the abyss of the Valley: a sheer cliff rising up to their right and a frightening drop to their left. They slowed to a stop and studied their predicament for a while. A long while.

'Why did the Indians quit chasing us, Juan?' Cooper asked, staring back along the steep trail. 'They had us dead to rights if they had kept on coming.'

'This place is forbidden,' Cortez sighed. 'Bad medicine to the Apache.'

'Forbidden to Indians, eh?' Bob Cooper almost smiled. 'That's pretty useful.'

'Not just Indians, Cooper, my friend.' The stare was cold and meaningful. 'We are in very big trouble if the stories are true.'

'What stories?' Cooper felt the sweat running down his spine as he sat nervously in his saddle watching the rider in front of him. 'What sort of stories are we talking about here?'

'They are just stories, *amigo*.' Cortez gently encouraged his stallion to start on the long descent down the narrow trail that led into the very jaws of Hell itself. 'We are not afraid of stories, right, *amigo*?'

'That depends, Juan Cortez.' Bob Cooper felt himself shaking as he sat in his tall saddle staring down at the steep trail and the even steeper drop to his left.

'You do not believe in ghosts, do you?' Cortez was laughing the way folks laugh when they are trying to make someone feel less concerned about a problem.

'Ghosts? Hell no.' Cooper wiped the sweat off his face. Suddenly the realization that they were no longer being fried by the burning sun came to the man. The shadows were a welcome bonus to himself and his lathered-up horse.

'Then follow me, Cooper,' Cortez said masterfully. 'We are not the first horsemen to use this trail today.'

'What you mean, Juan?'

'Study the ground,' Cortez answered. 'Many riders have torn up the ground very recently. I see shod and unshod tracks along this trail.'

'Unshod tracks?' Cooper rubbed his chin thoughtfully. 'I thought you said this place was out of bounds to our feathered friends, Juan?'

'I said that, did I not?' Cortez shook his head. 'This is most strange.'

Bob Cooper stared at the ground and saw the tracks beside his horse's hooves before shaking his reins so that his tired mount would follow the stallion once more. He gazed down at the incredible drop to his left. He had never been this far above solid ground before. It was like flying, although the lone hunter figured that no bird would ever fly this high. He was no longer feeling as safe now that he knew that Indians had ridden along this trail.

'You OK, *amigo*?' Juan Cortez called back to his silent friend.

'I hope so Juan.' Cooper swallowed hard and deep. 'I really hope so.'

The two horsemen slowly descended down the narrow trail following the tracks left by Cass and his men. It would be a long, slow journey that neither man would enjoy. The thought of the Apache war party at the mouth to the canyon trail above them kept the two riders heading down into the darkness.

Bob Cooper began to think about their situation. They were committed and there was no turning back. For the first time, he started to doubt the wisdom of his mission.

'You reckon that we might bump into any more Apache down here in the valley?' Cooper asked, as he steered his horse carefully along the delicate trail.

'I certainly hope not, my friend,' Cortez replied as he turned to face the man who was following him. 'This is not the place to try and fire one's pistols.'

'Very true,' Cooper gulped, staring into the abyss at his side as he clung to his reins.

THIRTEEN

Miguel Latoya sat astride his three-year-old mare that appeared to shine in the late afternoon sun, watching the desert that lay beyond the fertile valley dominated by the ranch belonging to Juan Cortez. The Cortez family had used the wide river that flowed through their land to cultivate the entire ranch and create a small paradise in an otherwise hostile land. Miguel, as well as other members of the Cortez household, was not used to being left behind when his master left this beautiful place. Miguel felt uneasy as he watched with eyes that were far sharper than any other member of the ranch workers. He seemed to be able to stare at nothing and yet see things that others could not envisage. Even the sun did not seem to stop the incredible eyesight of the man. His thick black eyebrows shaded his deep-set eyes so effectively that he appeared able to look directly into the sun at its brightest and not even seem troubled. There were those who said Miguel had been an eagle in a past incarnation.

Miguel patted the mare's neck as he studied the distant horizon and was troubled by what he saw. He had been gazing out into the white sand for over an hour and had not moved an inch from the spot. The horse just rested as her rider sat motionless in the large saddle. Miguel continued to remain perched like a buzzard awaiting something to die, as the sound of two horses gathered volume behind him. A quick glance over his shoulder confirmed his theory about who was riding up from the *hacienda*.

Slowly he returned his gaze to the distant horizon as Rosa Cortez reined in her palomino next to him, and the rotund Pedro Ramera puffed as heavily as his horse as he cantered to a halt.

Rosa looked her usual beautiful self in her riding clothes of black pants, white blouse and a slim-brimmed black hat as she sat atop the impressive golden horse, watching the heat-haze beyond the boundaries of their land.

'Miss Rosa, what are you doing here?' Miguel asked.

Rosa Cortez urged her palomino closer to the *vaquero*. 'What are you doing, Miguel?'

'I am glad you have come, Miss Rosa.' Miguel pointed at the far-off vista. 'That has been worrying me.'

Rosa and Pedro stared to where the man was indicating.

'I see nothing, Miss Rosa,' Pedro shrugged, rubbing his eyes as he failed to see anything. 'Do you see anything?'

'Quiet, Pedro.' Rosa Cortez leaned over and gripped Miguel by his shoulder forcing him to look at her. 'What do you see old one?'

'I see dust from many riders, Miss Rosa,' the man replied as he pointed at the distant dust that only he could see. Then he turned and pointed to his left. 'There is also more dust rising there.'

Rosa was puzzled. 'You mean that you can see two separate groups of riders, Miguel?'

Miguel nodded.

'Who are they, Miguel?' Pedro asked, pushing his sombrero off his sweating face. 'Can you make them out?'

'The first is an Apache war party heading toward the Valley of Death,' Miguel replied to his old friend.

'Isn't that where my brother was heading with Cooper?' Rosa sounded extremely distressed.

'*Si*, Miss Rosa.' Miguel looked into her eyes as if he were guilty of conjuring up the Indians.

'Who is making the second dust, Miguel?' Rosa tried to compose herself.

'I think that it must be riders from Don Jose Maldova's rancho.' The Mexican shrugged. 'It is coming from the right direction.'

91

'How can you be sure that is Apache?' She pointed to the first direction that he had indicated.

'I could see them earlier, but now they have ridden far away and all that remains is the dust rising from their ponies.' Miguel lifted his canteen and slowly unscrewed the top as he watched the sister of his master brooding over the information that he had imparted upon her young shoulders. She was distressed and full of questions that had no surefire answers.

'I do not like this, men,' she said in a cold, authoritative voice that neither man had heard before. 'Do you think that those Indians are after my brother and Cooper?'

'*Si*, Miss Rosa.' Miguel took a mouthful of water and then splashed some over his baked face. 'I think that those Indians are after Cooper and your brother.'

She pointed at the approaching dust-clouds. 'You will ride to intercept whoever is coming to our rancho, Pedro. Find out who it is and come straight back to me. 1 shall be at the *hacienda*.'

'*Si*, Miss Rosa.' Pedro kicked his horse hard and rode off toward the approaching riders.

Rosa Cortez slowly steered her horse around Miguel's and paused for a moment. 'Come with me, old one. We shall get all the able men from the rancho ready to ride.'

Miguel turned his mare. 'Ride where, Miss Rosa?'

The Valley of Death

'We are going to this Valley of Death that you speak of. We go to help Juan and Cooper.'

'Juan Cortez will not like it.' Miguel slapped his reins to follow her palomino as it started to race off back toward the *hacienda*. 'He will be very angry if we interfere.'

'They might end up very dead if those Indians catch up with them,' she shouted above the sound of her spirited horse's pounding hooves.

Cass led Holmes and Watkins ever onward along the narrow canyon at a steady pace. Then they heard a sound above them that chilled their bones. It was a noise unlike anything any of them had ever heard before.

It was the sound of warning that the Seri warriors always made when anyone was getting too close to their holy place. It was the sound that would wake the spirits and send the Seri the magic they required, the power that they knew was theirs and theirs alone. It was the sound that reminded the three riders of a million snakes hissing a final warning.

Holmes pulled up his mount. 'What the hell is that, Major?'

Cass turned his mount around and raised his Winchester to face the echoing rocks. 'Keep riding, men,' he ordered.

Watkins settled his horse and spurred on down the trail trying to escape the hauntingly eerie noise above their heads, but it was no use. Holmes grabbed frantically at the reins that held Green's horse that they were now using as a pack animal for their supplies. He gripped the leather and then spurred. Cass remained giving his men cover for a few seconds as he watched them galloping down the narrow draw. Just as he was about to turn his horse he saw the white images above him. They seemed to be everywhere. Major Jacob Harvey Cass had not experienced panic nor a sense of helplessness since the Battle of Gettysburg but now he felt a sudden rush of fear overwhelming him as he dug his spurs into the dumb animal's flesh.

As he rode after his men, he heard the noise rising again above his head. The sound was like that of snakes hissing and spitting their blinding venom over him. It was as if the air were filled with poison.

The arrows that rained down were long like the one that had passed through Fred Green's neck the previous evening. They seemed to be everywhere as they landed all around his charging battle-scarred horse. Cass heard the animal whinny in agony between his broad thighs as one of the arrows sank deeply into its flesh just behind the cantle of his saddle and the creature started to stumble then fall. Cass felt himself lifting over the horse's long, outstretched neck as the poor creature's legs began to buckle.

The Valley of Death

They both hit the ground hard and fast. Cass was somehow thrown clear and rolled up against a solid rock which ended his acrobatics. Regaining his senses, he cocked his Winchester that he still had gripped in his tired hands and fired up into the rocks at the white bodies that appeared to be racing around the lofty cliff face. He hit one, then two, as another volley of arrows made a dark cloud above him. It was like watching a massive swarm of hornets attacking as the arrows came hurtling down toward him.

Without thinking, the major threw himself at the prone, injured body of his horse avoiding the legs that were kicking at the air as its nervous system finally began to cease. He pulled himself as close as he could to the poor beast's body only a fraction of a second before the arrows started to hit the ground all around him. At least twenty of the long, lethal shafts hit the horse where it was lying as the renegade leader shuddered in terror.

The screaming hissing continued above his head coming from the countless warriors who were moving along small ridges. Cass finally exhaled and realized that he was still untouched by the deadly arrows. He pulled up his rifle as he stayed pinned down and primed the carbine once more and fired aimlessly. He was shooting blindly as he knew that he dare not risk raising his head above the bleeding body of his horse to take aim. Again and again he repeated the action, not knowing if his bullets were finding targets or not. It mattered little to the military man as he let shots off. It was as if he were trying to prove that he was still alive – if not to the Seri, then to himself.

All that concerned him as he lay in the steaming pool of blood that poured from the numerous arrow wounds in his dead animal was that he did not take one of those arrows. That he knew would be the end.

Major Jake Cass was not ready to die. Not now. Not when he had gotten so close to that which he sought. The treasure of this mystical place was going to be his. He had vowed that many years ago. No band of savages was going to stop him claiming his El Dorado this time.

Then he heard the spine-chilling sound of silence returning once more and he stopped firing. The Seri had stopped their devilish screaming for some unknown reason. Cautiously he edged his way along the length of the prostrate creature and peered up at the cliffs around him from under the stiff arrow-filled neck of his horse. They were gone again.

How could you fight an enemy that used such tactics, he thought to himself. This was indeed like doing battle with phantoms.

He lay for a few moments trying to think what to do next as he heard the sound of his men

returning along the narrow canyon, to assist
him. Cass got onto his knees and crawled back
down toward his saddle-bags and tried to release
them. The full weight of the dead horse was
bearing down on one side of his bags. He snarled
as he tried in vain to tug the bags free. It was no
use and he had to resign himself to the bitter
fact that all his pistol and rifle ammunition was
underneath the animal. He cursed for a moment
before concentrating upon the two riders who
were heading toward him leading the spare
horse.

'Get on Green's mount, Major,' Watkins yelled
down, as he gave cover with his Winchester as
Holmes pulled up to Cass who was scrambling
onto his feet. When the major had mounted, all
three men swung their horses around and
headed back along the trail.

'Thank you, men,' Cass said as he spurred the
horse alongside his two men. 'That was a real
brave thing for you to do.'

'We had to save you, Major,' Watkins shouted
back at his superior. 'Only you know the way out
of here.'

Even though they galloped, all three felt that
the snake men of the Seri would be wherever
they stopped.

FOURTEEN

If there ever was such a thing as a typical Mexican gentleman then Don Jose Maldova was it. He was a man who was closer to his sixth decade than his fifth and yet had an air about him that few younger men could equal. His neatly trimmed white beard contrasted against his tanned face and told tales of someone who had enjoyed his many years. When he mounted a horse, he somehow became part of that horse and rode with the strength of someone half his age. Don Jose was the elder statesman of the entire region and respected by all who knew him. He had a ranch of over a half-million acres south of Juan Cortez's ranch and seldom visited anyone except Cortez.

Having a small army of *vaqueros* he used them to escort him from one friend to another whenever the fancy took him. His main reason for visiting anyone though, was because he had an unmarried son named Luis. The only thing that drove Don Jose to embark on these long-distance visits to fellow ranchers was the fact that they all had daughters. Don Jose was a man who wanted grandchildren to inherit his vast properties.

Pedro Ramera led in the dozen or more *vaqueros* who surrounded Don Jose and his son Luis into the beautiful courtyard belonging to the Cortez family.

Don Jose sat in his saddle taking in the sweet fragrance-filled courtyard as he watched the petite figure of Rosa coming out of the large house to greet them. The old man with the elegant white trimmed beard studied the scene of all the Cortez men standing besides their horses and wondered what was happening in this usually peaceful place.

Rosa bowed as she approached the graceful man who was looking rather concerned. 'Don Jose. Welcome.'

'My dear Rosa.' He smiled, prompting his son into also greeting the beautiful female.

'Rosa,' Luis reluctantly nodded. Being the only child of an exceedingly wealthy man can make some great and others just a trifle selfish. Luis fell into the latter category.

'Luis.' Rosa stopped next to the head of Don Jose's horse and stroked its nose.

'Why are all your *vaqueros* ready to ride, Rosa?' Don Jose gestured with his arms at the

100

men before them. 'Do you have a problem?'

Rosa explained as Don Jose and his men entered the *hacienda* for refreshments whilst their horses were being watered. It was a story that made the old man very anxious as he listened intently to her tale. This was not what he had expected to greet him after such a long journey. This was not what he had come here for. This was a simple visit to attempt to get his son and his friend's sister interested in one another. Yet Don Jose Maldova was not a man to let mere diversions from his course worry him.

The elegant man finished his sherry and looked at his son over a long thin cigar. 'We ride with Juan Cortez's *vaqueros* to the Valley of Death so that we can help him.'

'Perhaps Juan does not wish us to interfere, Father?' Luis said, as he ran a finger along the brim of his black sombrero. 'I would hate for us to interfere.'

'Are you afraid of a few savages, my son?' Don Jose watched his offspring through the cloud of smoke that trailed from his lips.

'I? Afraid of Apache?' Luis did not make anyone believe anything different than that which they had already assumed.

'Bravo, Luis. Then we still ride to Juan's assistance, my son.' Don Jose smiled. 'We must try to help if we can.'

'Who is this *gringo* with your brother, Rosa?'

Luis stood before the lovely lady whose charms seemed to evade his senses.

'He is called Cooper, Luis,' Rosa answered.

Luis Maldova turned to his father. 'I do not like the idea of risking our *vaqueros* for a *gringo*, Father.'

'Cooper is a fine man.' Rosa snapped loudly, causing every male eye to focus upon her.

'I am sure he must be.' Don Jose bowed. 'Juan would not help a mere stranger if he did not see something good in his heart.'

'Exactly.' Rosa picked up her hat. 'Cooper is a real man like my brother.'

'Where are you going, little one?' the smiling Don Jose questioned.

'I ride to help Juan and Cooper.' Rosa's voice had surprise in its tone.

'You will stay here,' Luis said through pouted lips, as if he were addressing a child. 'This is not a job for a little girl.'

Rosa's face went almost crimson as she walked right up to the younger Maldova and started waving an angry finger under his nose. 'I am going, Luis. Do you not understand?'

Luis grabbed her hand and placed a kiss upon the tips of her fingers. It was not the kiss that comes from a lover to another lover, but the kiss of one who thinks he can take whatever he wishes. Simply because he wishes.

'You are not going without me,' Don Jose

shouted across at the tall man as he stroked his white beard with hands that were elegant in their length and shape.

'Release her, Luis,' Don Jose ordered. 'We are guests here in her home.'

The son did as the father commanded and leaned silently against the cool white wall as he rested his chin upon his chest and the frilly white shirt.

'I go with my men.' Rosa stormed from the *hacienda* and toward her waiting palomino. 'I go with my *vaqueros*, Don Jose. You can come with me or stay and drink more sherry. It is up to you.'

Don Jose and his men followed the female. She had mounted before they had reached their horses. 'May I and my *vaqueros* come with you, Rosa?'

'You may, Don Jose,' she grinned.

'This girl has fire in her belly, Luis,' Don Jose told his son as he mounted. 'She would make a good wife for the right man, I think.'

'She is very bossy, my father,' Luis grumbled as he stepped into his stirrup and hauled himself into his saddle. 'She will never get a husband unless she mends her ways and understands that men are the masters.'

'That is what you need,' Don Jose laughed. 'A woman who will control you.'

Rosa Cortez smiled and pulled her beautiful horse away from the hitching rail.

'Come on, *vaqueros*,' she shouted as her men mounted. 'We ride to find Juan and Cooper.'

Don Jose, his son, Luis, and his men rode after the galloping palomino and the *vaqueros* of Cortez. Soon all the valiant *vaqueros*, led by the young girl, would be thundering into the desert.

FIFTEEN

A mere mile from their last skirmish with the mysterious Seri warriors the two remaining renegades led by Major Cass were still riding with their Winchesters grasped tightly to their chests. Major Jake Cass had been riding the mount which once had belonged to their late companion Fred Green and was finding it very tough going. A horse can become like a favourite pair of boots and a rider gets used to the way his animal moves beneath him. Cass was not happy with the way Green's mount swayed as he galloped. Every mile felt like five on the seat of his pants but he was grateful that he had managed to escape death once more. The last ten minutes had become more and more frightening for the three weary men as they found themselves reaching the end of the long narrow trail. The canyon had been getting increasingly narrow as the three riders forged their way ahead since the unexpected Seri attack.

The sickening sight of two dead Apache and their ponies filled with the long arrows was not a sight that any of the trio welcomed as they passed the horrific scene. They slowed to a mere canter as they passed the bodies. Their horses started to become nervous as the aroma of rotting flesh filled their sensitive noses. It took experienced cavalrymen to control the terrified mounts as they rode past.

'Apache,' Cass said holding his hand before his mouth as he spoke in a surprised voice.

'What were Apache doing here, Major?' Watkins asked, as they rode past the bodies being consumed by flies. 'I thought that you said this place was bad medicine to most Indians?'

'It is bad medicine, Joe,' Cass replied holding his hand to his face as they travelled through the cloud of flies. 'I guess that even Indians can have their adventurous individuals.'

'What's that mean, Major?' the blond Cy Holmes queried.

'It means that even the Apache have their dumb critters just like us,' Watkins answered spurring his mount to get past the torrid place.

They rode fast for another half-mile before a sight rose up before them that caused more than a little despair. Now they were faced with a reality that forced them to pull their horses up to a stop. All three men squirmed in their saddles for what seemed an eternity.

The canyon seemed to end here. A rock face blocked any further riding. Now they had to dismount if they wished to continue. Jake Cass knew that they had to proceed because there was no turning back. Only he knew what this cave-like thing before them was: a hole carved by ancient rivers over a millennium was the only way forward for the three men. They stood beside their mounts staring at the hole and its black interior. It was like looking into the mouth of a cave but the major knew that this was no cave.

Cass remembered the last time he had been to the spot. Then he did not have his horse as it had been felled by a Seri arrow. He had had to walk through this desperate place avoiding the all-seeing eyes of the Seri snake people. He had done as they had done and used every rock to hide behind as he went. Cass recalled the sights ahead of them through the black natural passageway. Sights never seen by another white man and which made him swear that one day he would return and try to take the treasure back into civilization. It was so very long ago before all the blood and killings had filled all the empty parts of his brain's memory. Was it real or just a dream that had filled his young mind? Had the days of hiding without benefit of food and adequate drinking water made him just imagine the images that still seemed so real? Even Cass was not sure any longer as he stood clutching his rifle and reins. The hole in the rock face before them was a mere seven feet high and six feet wide at ground level.

'It's gonna be a tight squeeze, boys,' Jake Cass told his men as he automatically looked around the sheer cliff faces that seemed to hover over them.

'You want us to head into a cave, Major?' Watkins asked.

'It ain't a cave, Joe,' Cass sighed.

'It's a cave,' Holmes yelled. 'Look at it.'

Jake Cass faced the blond youth angrily and slapped him into silence. 'It ain't no damn cave, boy. I've been here before. It ain't no cave.'

Watkins and Holmes looked at their leader with eyes that were sore and swollen from lack of sleep. Neither man believed him but they were not willing to disagree with anything he said.

'Follow me.' Cass grabbed his mount's reins and led the horse into the blackness. Reluctantly, both his men trailed him with their mounts.

Single file was the order of the day as they edged their way into the strange, almost eerie darkness. This place had only one saving grace and that was that no Seri arrow could find them here within its black bosom.

It was so dark that it was difficult to believe it could be anything but a cave and yet Cass led them with his memory acting as scout. Wherever this place led it was at least better than what lay behind them. With every step the major took his memory became clearer as to what lay beyond this place of darkness.

It was as if light were being forced into his brain making him recall the place that he had long thought just a distant dream.

Jake Cass led his horse through the silence and cool natural passageway.

SIXTEEN

Juan Cortez stepped from his horse and stood silently watching the scene of carnage around him. Bob Cooper dismounted and led his horse until he was standing next to the taller man.

The sight of so many dead men, even though they were Apache, worried them. The dead ponies, too, did not sit well upon either man's stomach.

'This is not a sight that makes you want to have supper, my friend,' Cortez said removing his sombrero and crossing himself.

Cooper kept his Stetson on as he walked through the bodies with his horse following. 'We know that we're on the right trail anyway.'

'Only the renegades that you seek could have done this, Cooper.' Juan Cortez replaced his large hat and led his beautiful horse after the hunter. 'These Indians were hacked by a very large sword.'

'An officer's sabre,' Cooper corrected.

'*Si, amigo.*' Cortez placed his left boot into his stirrup and bounced back up on to his saddle. 'These men are evil.'

'You can say that again.' Cooper grabbed his saddlchorn and threw himself back on to his horse. 'How long can we continue before it gets dark?'

'We have a couple of hours,' Cortez replied as he studied the sky high above the towering walls on either side of them. Then he thought he saw something. '*Amigo?*'

'What, Juan?' Cooper looked at his friend and then diverted his eyes to where Cortez was staring. He squinted as he tried to make out what the Mexican was intrigued with. 'What did you see up there?'

'I am not sure,' Cortez said quietly. 'But whatever it was made me very frightened.'

Bob Cooper turned to face the man beside him. He had never seen a man's face so etched with troubled concern. 'You OK?'

Cortez jerked his stallion's reins to get its attention and rode up the small dune before them. The trail ahead became narrow again and he swung his horse about to face his friend who was following. 'Do you ever see something that you know cannot be?'

'What did you see up there?' Cooper asked firmly.

'It looked like a ghost, but I know that cannot

be,' Cortez shrugged as Cooper drew level with him once more.

'Let's ride,' Bob Cooper said standing in his stirrups, as his horse responded by charging forward away from the ugly scene of dead Indians. Juan Cortez kicked his stallion into action and raced past his friend. Both riders knew that this place held many secrets, most of which they had no desire to discover. The trail was a long one. The trail was also a narrow one. The rocks that towered over them seemed to have a thousand curious eyes. Eyes that followed them however far they journeyed, however fast they spurred their horses onward. Cooper and Cortez felt the hairs in the napes of their necks rising as they kept their horses moving until they came to a place that looked suitable enough to make camp. Reluctantly the two men decided to stop. This was not an ideal spot yet for many long hours they had been unable to find anywhere that looked as if it were safer than the next.

The sun had set and the darkness was getting ever more obvious and daunting. Their camp-fire lit up the sheer rocks around them and warmed their stiff bones, but could not wipe away the fear that they might not wake the following morning in this unholy place. Adding kindling to the rising flames before them both, Cooper and Juan Cortez said little to one another. Sometimes words can only add to a man's inner fears.

*

The darkness of night was the one thing that allowed the three men to survive as they finally emerged from the other side of the long tunnel set deep in the golden rock face. Major Jake Cass led his horse out into the fresh night air first and was quickly joined by his two nervous companions, Joe Watkins and Cy Holmes. They stood together in the black shadows that no moonlight seemed able to penetrate Holding the long leather reins of their bedraggled horses they could see but not be seen for the first time in the past two days.

Cass stood open-mouthed, staring across the wide level sand surface of the clearing that was ringed with the towering wall of the mysterious mountain. Soon his companions saw what he was gaping at and they, too, felt their jaws drop in wonder.

Before the trio of dangerous men, stood a massive edifice of unimaginable size. It was carved out of the gold-rich stone and stood five storeys high. Torches of flame covered the immense creation causing the gold ore to sparkle out across the otherwise barren place. No white man except Cass himself had ever set eyes upon this glorious structure before. It looked as if it had been constructed by skilled craftsmen and yet was the work of numerous generations of Seri braves who had carved this gigantic building into the mountainside itself. The torches' flames spiralled upwards before the beautiful creation like snakes dancing before their innocent prey. This was the place whose very existence was carved in legend itself and many had sought and many had failed to find, locating only disappointment and madness in the searching. This was truly a mirage and yet all three men knew what they were looking at: their eyes were fixed upon reality.

The eyes of the three men, as they stood in the dark shadows beside the tunnel were transfixed upon this unbelievable glittering myth.

Without realizing it all three men had moved forward into the centre of the clearing.

'What did I tell you, men?' Jake Cass said, as he sighed heavily taking in its wonders. 'A whole city carved out of solid gold.'

Joe Watkins rubbed his tired eyes. 'Is it real?'

'Sure looks real to me, Joe,' Cy Holmes sighed in awe. 'What is it?'

'El Dorado,' Cass laughed. 'I told you, didn't I?'

'You sure did, Major.' Watkins blew out the day's exhaustion as he tried to take in the entire thing. It was too vast for any human eyes to comprehend in one go.

'And it's filled with gold and jewels.' Cass licked his dry lips as if tasting the wealth before them. 'More jewels and gold than anyone could ever imagine. It's all ours. Ours.'

Their greed had only a few moments to develop before the three men were suddenly brought back into the blinding reality of their situation. A sound started quietly and slowly built up into a deafening crescendo. It was the hissing sound that had haunted them earlier. Now it was all around them, encircling them in its terrifying regularity.

It was Cass who was first to react and search the surrounding cliff wall with his aching eyes. Then his two remaining men drew their weapons as they, too, looked about the area, trying to see the faces that were making the bloodcurdling racket.

Watkins and Holmes led their horses into the middle of the flat area toward the carved building following the long solid steps of their leader. They felt like gladiators waiting for the lions to be released into the arena of some ancient Roman amphitheatre.

Slowly they began to notice the Seri warriors in their white body paint appearing from everywhere around them. Even the tunnel behind them began to echo with the sound as braves moved down the route that had led them to this place. The only place that these small strange people did not seem to be, was the huge carved building itself. Cass kept walking his horse toward the golden torch-illuminated place with his two trusty allies beside him.

'Oh my God,' Watkins gulped. 'Look at them.'

'Major?' Holmes started to scream as he could see the small white bodies appearing all about them. 'There are thousands of them, Major.'

Jake Cass drew his sabre. 'Steady, men. Don't panic, just keep walking.'

To keep walking was far easier to say than actually do as the major knew only too well. It was a long trek across the level manicured sand toward the incredible vision. Yet, the man with the sabre knew that he had one job to do and that was lead by example. Nothing could prevent him leading his motley crew whilst he still had blood flowing in his veins. Whilst he led his men would follow and that was the only thing all three still retained from the days when they were real soldiers.

The noise became even louder than any of the three thought possible as the Seri continued their warning shrilling.

'We're almost there,' Cass panted as he pulled his horse along toward the torchlight. 'Just keep moving. Keep moving.'

Joe Watkins stumbled as he tried to keep pace with his leader but would not allow himself to remain upon the ground for the Seri to find with their long arrows. Holding his pistol in one hand and the reins in the other he somehow managed to scramble onto his feet to continue following Cass.

Cy Holmes tried to stay close to the major as fear swept over the young man. He had lost any sense of reason and was simply unable to do anything any longer except follow orders. His was a mind starved of rational thought. Now he was living amid his own hysterical fear. All he could see were the white ghost-like figures above and around them as they proceeded.

'Major Cass,' Holmes whined. 'We are trapped.'

'Keep walking and don't fire unless they start something, Cy,' Cass ordered. 'Hear that, Joe?'

Watkins was almost running as he tried to keep pace with the major. 'I hear you but I don't like it.'

'As long as they hold off with them arrows of theirs we're OK.' Jake Cass felt his own perspiration trickling down his face from under his hat brim and realized that he too was far more worried than he liked. 'OK?'

'OK,' Holmes stammered.

'OK, Major,' Watkins gasped as their pace increased. 'But I could nail a few of them.'

'Do that and we are all finished.' Cass snapped. 'We got eighteen rounds between us before we have reload. How many Indians can you see?'

All three men were still looking at the golden monster before them as they noticed the warriors starting to come down on to the flat central sandy area from the rocks. There had to be at least several hundred visible already and more coming by the still deafening noise around the towering mountains. Jake Cass had never been in such a fix as this. This was not like anything he had ever experienced before. The last time he had ventured into this place he had been alone, the last survivor of a doomed group of adventurers. He had escaped because he had been able to slip away from these people unnoticed. Days of hiding during daylight hours and nights of clambering over mountains that almost touched the stars themselves. Now it was different. Now it was totally different. He wondered to himself whether he would have returned to this evil place had he known there were so many of these strange Seri. Before he could find an answer within his own soul they had reached the foot of the carved monster that resembled a building.

'Now what, Major?' Watkins asked, holding his reins tightly.

'Get your rifles and saddle-bags,' Cass commanded, sliding his Winchester from its sheath and ripping off the saddle-bags that had once belonged to Fred Green. He had no idea of their contents but secretly prayed they held ammunition for his handgun and rifle.

When both men had their bags and carbines they followed the gaunt figure up a flight of stone carved steps to the second level. So far they had seen no Indians on this structure but they kept a watchful eye as the major knelt behind a solid stone pillar to catch his breath. Holmes and Watkins joined him as they surveyed the scene below and around them.

'How many Indians are there?' Holmes asked, as tears rolled down his cheeks.

'Too many, Cy,' Cass muttered, touching the young man's shoulder. 'Too many.'

SEVENTEEN

The Seri seemed unlike any other tribe the three men had ever encountered. These were a people with a mission and they had almost religious dedication to their task. Whatever the true reason for their being in this remote place, Jake Cass and his two comrades would never discover. All they could hope for was to live a little longer through the long dark night. Slowly the three ex-Confederate soldiers made their way up across the colossal carved building, never stopping longer than a few seconds as they studied the scene before them. Although impossible, they tried to estimate how many warriors had them pinned down on this priceless rock.

'I reckon there's at least five hundred,' young Cy Holmes said, as they reached the third storey with their rifles and saddle-bags in tow.

'I figure more,' Joe Watkins sighed rubbing his eyes. 'A lot more.'

Major Jake Cass sat with his spine against a

massive pillar unbuckling the straps of Fred Green's saddle-bags upon his belly, hoping he would find some boxes of shells for either his pistol or his Winchester. 'You boys sure figure big for two fellas who never got past ninth grade.'

'I can count, Major,' Holmes said, as he watched the Indians below them filling the level clearing. 'I can count real good.'

Cass was just about to say something else when his eyes fell upon a surprise that had been hidden in the saddle-bags.

'What's the matter, Major?' Watkins asked seeing the strange expression upon his leader's face.

'Nothing's wrong, Joe,' Jake Cass grinned. 'In fact everything's fine. Just fine.'

Both Holmes and Watkins watched the older man as he dug a hand into either bag. From one he pulled fuses and the other he withdrew sticks of dynamite.

'Dynamite,' Cy Holmes gasped. 'Where did that come from?'

'Fred's saddle-bags, Cy,' Cass laughed.

'What was old Fred doing with dynamite?' Watkins asked curiously.

For a moment Jake Cass concentrated. 'Remember that bank we were going to rob in Sante Fe a year or so back?'

'Yep,' Watkins nodded.

'Remember we called off the job at the last moment?' Cass had counted more than a dozen sticks of the explosive in the leather bag. 'Fred got the dynamite for that job and we never had cause to use it.'

'So he hung onto it?' Holmes gave a whistle. 'Was he stupid or what? I would never have rode around with that stuff behind my ass.'

Cass chuckled. 'It's lucky for us that Fred was an idiot.'

'How come?' Watkins was tired as he asked the question.

'We got a way of getting out of this tight spot.' Cass smiled at his two weary men. 'We blast our way out.'

'We do?' Holmes felt uneasy.

'Yeah. We do.' Jake Cass placed the sticks back into the saddle-bags and got onto his knees and peered down. 'I figure these Seri tribesmen have never experienced dynamite before. It will be an education for the critters.'

'Ain't dynamite a little dangerous, Major?' Cy Holmes asked, as he felt the sweat rolling down his spine again. 'We might blow ourselves up.'

'I'll handle the dynamite. Don't fret your-selves.' Jake Cass gave a sigh as he looked at the bag full of long sticks. It was the one thing he had not expected to find. He had hoped for bul-lets but dynamite could be a lot better in the long run.

Watkins sighed wearily. 'What you thinking about, Major?'

'We gotta get ourselves some of this treasure before we leave tomorrow,' the major said.

'How much we gonna take?' Holmes asked innocently.

'We'll just fill our saddle-bags,' Cass grinned. 'That ought to be enough to make us very rich varmints.'

'Sounds good,' Watkins yawned.

'Sounds real good,' Holmes smiled.

Cass watched the hundreds of eerie people below them, painted from head to toe in a white-wash substance. The man could not truly believe his eyes but had to. These Seri braves were there all right. Like living ghosts. Defiant.

'Ghosts,' he muttered.

'Shucks, Major. Don't start talking about ghosts again. It gives me the creeps,' Watkins muttered, as he tried to keep his eyes open.

'You boys get some shut eye,' Cass said as he stood guard over his small army. 'I'll wake you if any trouble starts.'

'What sort of trouble, Major?' Holmes gulped.

'If we gets killed, I'll let you know first,' Cass said dryly.

'You shouldn't josh like that, Major.'

'Just sleep, Cy.' Jake Cass rested his chin on the cold barrel of his carbine as he watched the people below. Then he realized something.

The ear-splitting shrieking had ceased. Now silence hushed the entire area and it was a silence that made Cass uneasy. The stars above were bright as the moon hid beneath a long black cloud. Only the light that emanated from the huge torches dotted over the massive carved building lit up the scene before him. It seemed to dance its orange glow across each and every white-stained face of the braves, faces that seemed to show no signs of humanity. Cass pondered whether the faces were as dead without the white paint as they were with it. The major had time now to rest in his own thoughts as his men fell into sleep at his feet. He started to remember those long gone days again when he had last come to this place. Then he had seen only a handful of Seri warriors. To face such a show of strength had shaken him right down to his cavalry boots. He had never imagined that there were so many of the secretive creatures hidden in and around this place. Yet there they were standing defiantly below him holding their bows and arrows proudly. Unafraid. He had seen bravery many times during his army days but the valour the Seri displayed made him respectful of their courage. It was difficult to imagine what was running through the minds of such a primitive people. Then he cast his eyes about him over the heads of his two men as they rested. The structure that they were hiding upon was carved by these Indians. It was not the work of savages; it was the work of skilled craftsmen.

Nothing made sense in this place. Cass would wait for the sun to rise before doing anything as long as the Indians remained where they were.

He swallowed deeply as he wondered if *they* would remain where they were. A sudden attack seemed unlikely but he put no heed in his gut feelings where the Seri were concerned.

EIGHTEEN

The overnight ride had not prevented Rosa Cortez, Don Jose and Luis Maldova and the *vaqueros* from continuing their long quest toward the place they knew as the Valley of Death. Led by Miguel Latoya whose sharp eyes were their only real advantage over the Apache braves they knew were somewhere ahead in the desert, the riders denied themselves sleep in order to catch up with Bob Cooper and Juan Cortez.

Rosa rode as well as any man and upon her palomino she was matchless. The spirit of the sixteen-year-old female was far superior to any of the men who rode with her. She was driven by love; love of a brother and the greater love of a man for whom she felt strongly, gave her the willpower to overcome any physical difficulties.

Luis Maldova rode only because his father had instructed him to do so. Over the hours he had managed to allow his horse to fall to the back of the group of riders. He had absolutely no intention of being the first to meet the Apache.

Then, as the sun was starting to rise and the sky became coloured with an orange hue, Miguel Latoya raised an arm and pulled his mount to a stop.

Rosa drew her palomino alongside Miguel. 'What is it?'

'Apache.' Miguel pointed ahead into the distance.

The other riders all came to a stop behind the pair as they talked.

'How many, Miguel?' Rosa asked, as she watched the man studying the desert ahead. It was still too dark for anyone else to see anything but the man beside Rosa saw clearly.

'Ten,' he answered confidently.

'Ten Apache?' Luis Maldova said in a voice that did not sound as masculine as he would have liked.

'Yes, *amigo*.' Miguel turned to the fearful man in the fancy clothes. 'Ten. Only ten.'

'That is a lot, Rosa,' Don Jose said soundly. 'One Apache is the same as five of us.'

'Do not be stupid, Don Jose,' Rosa snapped. 'They are just men. We are more. We can defeat them.'

Pedro Ramera rode closer to the young maiden. 'I do not like the Apache, Miss Rosa.'

'Be brave, fat one,' Rosa said, smiling. 'We are

vaqueros and we will be victorious.'

Luis Maldova moved his horse closer to his father. 'I wish to go home, Father.'

'Quiet, Luis,' Don Jose ordered.

Rosa started to count the heads in her group of riders. 'I see we have eighteen guns against those Indians.'

'*Si*, Miss Rosa,' Miguel agreed. 'We could ride in making lots of noise and shooting. That might frighten the Indians away.'

'That is good.' Rosa slapped Miguel on his back. 'You are a mighty *vaquero*, Miguel.'

'He is loco,' Pedro shrugged.

Miguel turned dramatically to the assembly of horsemen. 'The Apache are sleeping. Only one brave is awake near the ponies. If we make a lot of gunfire I think they will flee.'

The riders seemed to agree with the eagle-eyed one as they talked amongst themselves, with the one exception of the younger Maldova.

'Are your guns loaded?' Rosa asked.

The men all drew their pistols and made a positive noise that filled her heart with satisfaction.

'Then we ride, *vaqueros*.' Rosa drew her own gun and raised it high above her head firing a single shot into the morning air.

All eighteen riders started toward the Indian encampment noisily firing shots into the air and shouting at the top of their lungs. Their gunfire filled the chilly air with frightening noise. Even Luis rode with them although he rode slower than anyone else. Just in case.

The riders knew that they were taking a chance by attacking the sleeping Apache but it had to be done. When the startled braves awoke they wondered what was happening. With the low bright sun on their backs, the riders charged making the most terrifying sound that they could manage.

Unable to tell what was happening, the warriors quickly grabbed their ponies and threw themselves onto the backs of the nervous animals. Within a few minutes the entire hunting party of Apache had galloped north in a vain attempt to regroup and evaluate the situation.

Rosa and her men rode over the discarded blankets and on toward the place that they knew Cooper and Juan Cortez had been heading.

The Apache drew together and watched as the *vaqueros* thundered past them. They waited for a long while before returning to their destroyed camp. They cautiously retrieved the few remaining weapons that were not trampled beyond repair before heading off into the desert and their far off stronghold. Today the white eyes had won the day: tomorrow however was another matter.

NINETEEN

The moment that Bob Cooper and Juan Cortez felt the long arrows prodding their sides they awoke. The sight that their sleep-filled eyes perceived made their blood run cold.

At least a dozen or more of the white-painted figures hovered above them aiming their deadly bows at them where they lay. This was no way to greet a new day. Yet this was the way that these strange Seri warriors had decided it would start for both Cooper and Cortez.

Lying on their backs they knew that they were not going to be able to get out of this situation alive if they attempted to fight. Every arrow in every bow was aiming at them, ready to be released if they even blinked aggressively.

'I think we are in trouble, *amigo*,' Juan Cortez said in an almost humorous way.

'I think we are in big trouble, Juan,' Cooper agreed.

The Seri braves stepped backward and indicated that the men rise. Both men obeyed cautiously. Standing they towered above the small band of strange tribesmen, none of whom could have been more than five feet in height.

'Cunning little devils,' Cortez smiled as he watched his and Cooper's gunbelts being taken from them. 'I think they have a slight advantage over us.'

'What you reckon they intend doing?' Cooper asked his pal.

'They could have killed us but they did not, *amigo*.' Cortez made a face that suggested thought. 'I think they might be just going to torture us or something.'

'That's cheered me up,' Cooper sighed. He had never felt so helpless before and did not like it.

Jake Cass had awoken his two men at the first hint of sun as it started to break over the tall mountains. The Seri were still filling the level area before them as they took refuge on the massive carved structure. As the morning sunshine hit the carved frontage the glittering of gold sparkled out across the scene.

'This place is made of solid gold, Major,' Watkins said as he gathered up his saddle-bag and passed out the last of his jerky between them.

'This mountainside must be riddled with seams of gold and when they carved out this temple, or whatever it is, it just sorta made it kinda special, men,' Cass said looking about them.

'When we going inside to find them jewels, Major?' Cy Holmes asked, as he took a chunk off his strip of jerky and began chewing.

Cass stared down at the Seri below them, then waved at his two men. 'Empty whatever you got in your bags and go in now. Fill them up with what you can find.'

'What about you, Major?' Watkins asked.

'I'll keep an eye on these Indians.' Cass chewed on his less than satisfying breakfast.

'You shout if you needs us,' Joe Watkins said, as he emptied the few remaining objects from his bag. There was not much to show for all the years of following the major. Holmes did the same and then both men ran doubled up into the huge carved entrance of the building.

Jake Cass sat flicking his hand through the objects on the ground before him. A half-full box of shells for the Winchesters and another box of .45 calibre bullets for their pistols. It was not as good as he had expected. He tried to calculate how many rounds each they had but decided that it was too few to bother.

Only the dynamite gave them any chance of escape and he knew it. They would have to somehow blast their way out from this place with their booty. To attempt to shoot their way out would leave them running out of ammunition after only a few minutes.

Cass rubbed his neck as he considered the problem before him.

'We are up against it this time,' he muttered aloud to himself.

Within the huge building on the third level, Joe Watkins and his younger companion walked around in awe of what they saw. This was a place filled with such wealth that it would take an entire regiment to empty this one room alone. Yet they were only two with a saddle-bag each. Where to start was their biggest problem as they strolled slowly around the solid gold statues and jewelled objects that were everywhere, jars filled to the brim with diamonds and every other sort of gem known to the pair.

'What are these red stones?' Holmes asked his friend, as he held out a palm filled with rubies.

'Beats me,' Watkins shrugged, as he himself found a casket full to overflowing with diamonds. 'They looks valuable though.'

'Shall we just take the stones or should we take some of the golden things as well?' Holmes was looking at small golden statues.

'Both,' Watkins said as he started to fill his bags with the wealth before him.

The two men took only a matter of minutes to fill the saddle-bags with the precious gems and solid gold objects before them. They buckled the bags and then dragged them across the floor and out into the sunshine back to the waiting major who was crouching behind the small wall staring down at the crowd. As they reached his side they dropped the bags and gazed over the edge of the wall.

'What's happening, Major?' Watkins asked, as he became aware of the turmoil below.

'Something's sure happening, Joe,' Cass said thoughtfully. 'I wish I knew what.'

Holmes gazed down and it was he who first noticed activity at the small tunnel entrance that they had used to get into this secret place. Indians were rushing into the tunnel and then back out as if doing something imperative.

'What do your young eyes see, Cy?' Cass asked the blond man next to him.

'I reckon that they have captured something, Major,' Holmes answered slowly.

'What could they have captured?' Watkins scratched his head as he tried to think.

Cass straightened up as a sight befell his tired eyes. 'Do you see what I see, men?'

'I see something.' Watkins rubbed his face as if it might help his vision.

'They done caught a couple of people,' Cy Holmes gasped in total surprise. 'White people.'

'That has to be the varmint who's been on our tail for the past two years,' Cass grinned as he studied the Seri dragging the two men out of the tunnel and into the vast clearing.

'The hunter?' Watkins grabbed the major's arm.

'Yeah. They caught the hunter and what looks like a Mexican.' Cass laughed quietly. 'They caught the ghost.'

'Ghost?' Watkins queried.

'Well he's been damn well haunting us for a couple of years, ain't he?' Cass was now on his feet and shaking with laughter as he watched the Seri pulling their two captives into the centre of the huge level area. The white-stained warriors parted as the two captives were forced along.

'What they gonna do with them, Major?' Holmes asked.

'Torture seems a good bet, Cy,' Cass grinned.

Then it started again. The sound of hissing. The hissing of snakes that came from the Seri braves' throats Soon every single one of the Indians was making the same nerve-breaking sound and relishing in it as it echoed around this strange mystical place.

The hairs on the backs of Cass's and his two men's necks started to rise as the noise reached its chosen targets. The three men on the holy structure were the ones that these small creatures were trying to frighten, not the two that they had their arrows aimed at.

Even these primitive ancient people could tell

the difference between good and evil. Their
shrilling noise increased in volume for what
seemed an endless time to the trio upon the
golden building.

'They'll kill him for us, Major,' Watkins said to
his superior.

'Yeah.' Jake Cass pondered as if he wanted to
do the job himself. 'If that is him, Joe.'

'What ya mean, Major?' Watkins cautiously
stood beside the older man. 'Who else could it
be?'

Cass swung his head around and gazed hard
into Watkins's face for a moment. 'I just wondered if it might be someone else.'

'It don't matter who they are.'

'It does to me, Joe,' Cass mumbled clenching
his fists. 'I wanna know if that's the critter who's
been trailing us for two years.'

'Why?' Holmes puzzled.

'So I can sleep at night,' Cass replied. 'If that
ain't the man who has been following our every
step, then that means he's still out there some-
place.'

'Waiting.' Watkins nodded.

'Exactly,' Cass snarled. 'Waiting. Waiting to
gun us down when we least expect it.'

'It has to be him.' Cy Holmes waved his hands
about. 'Who else could it be?'

'The man who's trailing us ain't got no
Mexican with him.'

Cy Holmes stood beside the pair and he, too, started to stare down at the hundreds of figures below them. 'Yeah, it might just be someone else.'

'If it is,' Cass breathed heavily, 'we could fight our way out of this place only to run smack into the hunter.'

All three men stood watching the scene below them and thought long and hard. What to do? What to do?

TWENTY

It was as if fate thought it might just step in and assist the three renegades who seemed unable to make a decision. For no sooner had the three men stood upright on the third level of the temple carved out of golden rock, than the sound of hissing started to come from within the structure as well as the mouths of the Seri warriors below.

Jake Cass turned to face the dark, carved entrance that his two followers had just walked through with their saddle-bags full to overflowing with gems and gold; the sound seemed to be coming from inside.

'It's just an echo, Major,' Watkins said confidently, touching the older man's sleeve.

'I think not.' Cass drew his sabre and strode forward to the large entrance. He stood waiting for his eyes to adjust to the darker interior.

'We just came out of there, sir,' Holmes said. 'There ain't no Indians in there.'

Cass stood motionless holding his sabre raised. He listened and waited. Then he saw something that he had not expected. It was not Seri braves hissing loudly this time; it was snakes.

'Damn,' Cass stammered in surprise. 'Snakes.'

Watkins and Holmes rushed to their leader's side and they, too, were shocked at the sight that met them. Snakes. Snakes that seemed to be coming from everywhere. Dozens, then hundreds of snakes were appearing from behind the golden statues. Slithering over the tables that were covered in precious gems and all heading for the sunlight behind the three men.

'Snakes, Major,' Holmes shrieked in horror. 'Hundreds of them. What we gonna do?'

Cass used his sabre to good effect and a few well-placed blows killed the first to reach him. Then there were too many of them. He backed away with his two men at his side. The snakes seemed to be appearing from everywhere on this great structure they stood on.

'What we gonna do, Major?' Watkins asked, as they reached the three saddle-bags.

Jake Cass stared around them as more and more poisonous serpents appeared from every small cavity along the carved stone ledge leading toward the upper levels of the structure. He plucked up the bag at his feet containing the dynamite and gritted his teeth. 'We better try and get to the horses.'

His two men grabbed their heavy bags full of wealth and followed the man as he led the way down. Only his gleaming sabre forged a route through the venomous creatures as he carved out a path by chopping the snakes that were before him. His arm ached as he swung it continuously back and forth slicing the angry creatures away from their escape route down to the flat surface of this secret place. When they reached the first level they leapt over the remaining snakes into the soft sand. As they rose to their feet they faced the seemingly endless numbers of white-painted figures before them. Quickly Cass slid his sabre into its scabbard as they got to their feet and found the horses.

'Joe. You hold them horses steady so they don't lit out without us,' Jake Cass yelled over the sound of the hissing Seri braves.

Watkins slung his saddle-bags over his horse and tied it up behind the cantle of his saddle. 'Right, Major.'

Holmes grabbed his horse and placed the heavy bag on to the creature's hind quarters. 'What you gonna do, sir?'

Cass slung the bags over his shoulder and pulled out a stick of dynamite and a long fuse. 'Carve us a way outa here, son.'

The two men mounted their horses and held the reins real tight as Joe Watkins also held the major's horse in check as they watched the older man striking a match and setting the fuse alight.

Major Jake Cass stood holding the stick of explosives for what seemed an eternity to Watkins and Holmes. The major seemed to be waiting for the fuse to get as low as possible before deciding to toss it. When it was a mere three inches from the stick of dynamite he threw it high into the air above the heads of the hundreds of Seri.

The explosion was so violent that its impact seemed to cut a massive gap in the ranks of the warriors. At least several dozen were lying lifeless before the three renegades as Cass mounted his horse and laid his bags across the neck of his horse before he pulled out another stick and fused it quickly before the braves had time to react.

'Got a smoke, Joe?' Cass asked.

Watkins dug out the remains of a cigar from his vest pocket and offered it to the man beside him.

'Light it, Joe,' Cass ordered watching the stunned faces before him.

The cigar was lit and handed to the major who blew at the hot end of the smoke before touching it to the fuse. Once it had started to burn furiously he put the cigar between his teeth and gripped it. 'This ain't gonna be easy.'

'There are too many of them,' Holmes noted nervously. 'We are gonna get carved up, Major.'

'I hope not,' Cass said tossing the dynamite into the heart of the warriors before them. The ground seemed to quake beneath their horses' hooves as it exploded furiously, sending men flying into the air amid the debris of earth and body parts. The undaunted Seri were starting to back away from the man with the exploding sticks as Cass gently spurred his horse forward. The gigantic structure towered over the three riders and vibrated from the aftershocks of the explosion, sending vipers falling from its walls. Diamondbacks and sidewinders littered the ground around the three men's horses, spitting their venom in all directions.

Suddenly a pitiful scream rang out from behind the major and Watkins causing the two men to turn and watch as the young Cy Holmes clung to his saddlehorn trying to stay on his nervous mount. The snakes were all around the hooves of the terrified beast as the horse leapt into the air trying to avoid their merciless fangs. Soon they were sinking their deadly teeth deep into the legs of the beast every time the creature came back down to earth. Holmes, like his two companions was an experienced cavalryman but even he could not control an animal that was being bitten and filled with the juice of death. 'Major!'

Cass watched helplessly as the younger man's horse started to reel uncontrollably in a spinning motion before finally falling victim to the virulent brew that surged through its veins. The blond man rolled off the beast as it violently crashed into the ground. Lying silently for a second, Holmes opened his dazed eyes. The sight that met him caused his heart to beat even faster than it was already doing. The snakes were now turning their attention towards him. 'Major!' he cried as he started to get to his feet.

Cass and Watkins watched as the snakes coiled and sprang at the man sinking their fangs deep into his flesh releasing their deadly venom into his body. The major knew that it was too late to help the man as he fought to control his own horse as it nervously skipped away from the sight.

'We gotta do something, Major,' Watkins yelled at his grim-faced mentor.

There was only one thing to do and the major knew he had to do it. Drawing his Army Colt hesitantly from its holster, he aimed at the young man who was vainly trying to fend off the attacks from the snakes.

'Major?' Joe Watkins looked at his superior with eyes that had seen this desperate action before.

'I gotta do this, Joe,' Cass screamed as he aimed carefully at the head of Cy Holmes then

144

fired. It was over with one accurate shot that ended the man's agony. The body fell next to the stricken horse.

'What about the saddlebags, Major?' Watkins asked, as he held on to his reins tightly. 'We gonna leave them?'

'We still got one bag, Joe,' Cass shouted. 'Ain't that enough?'

Watkins held on to his horse as the major lit another fuse and tossed the dynamite stick at the warriors before them. The blast sent a cloud of acrid smoke swirling around the once sacred clearing before them.

'They never seen dynamite before, Major,' Watkins said, with his rifle across his chest. 'They don't know what it is.'

'I just hope we got enough sticks to get to the tunnel, boy,' Cass said as he pulled a fourth stick and fuse out from his bag.

The two horses edged their way ahead as the warriors parted before them still holding onto their bows.

'We gotta get to the tunnel fast,' Cass snarled with the cigar in his teeth.

Then the braves started to raise their primed bows. A couple at first, then more. Soon every arrow was aimed at the two riders as they cautiously made their way towards the centre of the clearing. Bob Cooper and Juan Cortez were left alone as the Seri warriors retreated away from

the two men and the exploding sticks. Cooper
and his friend stood watching the approaching
riders as they encroached ever closer.

Suddenly a thunderous volley of long arrows
left the bows of the white-stained Indians. The
sound was like a million hornets as the deadly
artillery found their mark. Cass's horse reared
into the air as it felt the agony of the arrows pen-
etrating its flesh. Cass fell backwards onto the
ground as he watched his remaining companion
being ripped apart before his eyes. The arrows
tore Joe Watkins and his horse to shreds. What
fell to the ground beside him was little more
than meat. Even the battle-experienced Jake
Cass had never seen such a sight as he rolled
over wondering what to do next. Then he saw the
two men standing before him.

The look in Bob Cooper's face chilled Cass's
blood. For the first time in his long, futile life he
was facing a man who had good reason to hate
him. For the first time he had to face a man who
sought vengeance for the past.

Cortez remained where he had been standing
since being brought into this place by the Seri
warriors. His black eyes watched in shock as the
Indians made a huge circle around the two white
men in their midst. Cooper and Cass were alone
to face one another. The trouble was that Cooper
was unarmed and Jake Cass still had his pistol
resting in his holster, as well as his trusty sabre

hanging from his hip. Juan Cortez knew that it was pointless saying anything about the odds not being even to these strange little warriors as they would never understand him.

Bob Cooper moved towards the man who was suddenly feeling like a caged animal. 'So you're the swamp scum who killed my wife and child?'

Jake Cass gritted his teeth as he tried desperately to compose himself. There had been so many killings he found it hard to differentiate between them. 'You are the ghost.'

'I ain't no ghost.' Cooper felt himself being drawn towards the creature who only just scraped in as a human being. As he moved he looked at the silent Indians who surrounded them and wondered who were the true savages. Certainly not these small-framed people who had not sought the violence that had been forced upon them.

'Maybe I'll alter that.' Jake Cass drew his sabre and raised it against the morning sunshine. The flashing light that reflected off the honed blade was like lightning.

Bob Cooper seemed oblivious that he was walking towards certain death, as he continued to approach the glazed eyes and ruthless expression of Major Jacob Cass. 'What you gonna do?'

Cass seemed almost nervous by the attitude of the Montana rancher and his icy stare. 'Stay back or I'll slice you in two.'

'Ya think I care?' Cooper drawled, as he noticed the man moving slowly backwards trying to maintain the distance between them. 'What can you do to me?'

'I can kill you,' Jake Cass replied angrily.

'You did that two years ago.' Bob Cooper removed his Stetson and tossed it away.

Cass started to swing his sabre excitedly. 'I warned you to stay your distance.'

Cooper walked after the retreating ex-officer. 'You scared of fighting me without your weapons?'

Jake Cass stopped and thrust the sabre into the soil at his feet before unbuckling his gunbelt and draping it over the hand guard of his gleaming sword. 'I ain't been afraid of nothing for years, sonny.'

Cooper watched as the man removed his large coat and allowed it to fall onto the ground behind him.

'Now we are even,' Cass snarled. 'That good enough for you, boy?'

Cooper stopped moving and glanced around the many faces that made up the silent warriors before staring at the tall Juan Cortez. Cooper nodded at the Mexican as if telling him something with a simple look that no amount of words could convey. Juan Cortez removed his sombrero and crossed himself before returning the nod.

Cooper returned his attention to the Confederate renegade and found himself smiling. 'Good enough.'

The two men charged into each other with as much force as they could muster. The resulting impact caused both to crash into the ground with hands at each other's throats before Cooper found himself taking solid punches to the jaw. Cass, unlike his enemy, was used to killing with or without weapons. All that Bob Cooper had going for him was a burning fire in his guts, the burning fire of revenge.

Finding strength from a place deep within himself, Cooper forced the heavier man off and smashed a mighty blow into his face. Blood flowed from a gash over the major's left eye as he returned the punches with twice as much ferocity.

Cooper felt himself passing out from the sheer force of the blows as he desperately tried to crawl away. A rain of punches followed him as he felt himself slipping into the blackness of oblivion as knuckles found his face.

Cooper clenched a right fist and hit the man as hard as he could in the ribs. Cass rolled over and scrambled back to his feet. Then he kicked Cooper with such force that the younger man lifted off the ground and found himself on his knees.

'You're a dead man,' Jake Cass screamed, wiping the blood off his face as he walked back to his sabre and pulled it from the soil. 'Whoever you are, you're gonna meet your Maker.'

Bob Cooper coughed desperately, attempting to get his wind back as he saw the awesome figure approaching with the glinting sword in his hands. He tried in vain to get to his feet but found himself falling head first back onto the ground again. The weary eyes of the lone hunter watched helplessly as Cass moved ever closer.

Jake Cass paused above the man who lay gasping for air at his feet, raising the deadly blade above his head. 'You ain't gonna haunt me any more, sonny.'

Cooper lay watching the man through blurred eyes when he suddenly noticed the expression change upon Cass's face.

Major Jake Cass found himself suddenly aware of the scores of silent Seri braves around them. They no longer held their bows passively at their sides but had raised them. Now the sadistic soldier found himself ready to strike the final death blow to the helpless Bob Cooper, yet he could not stop himself from looking at the painted faces of the small Indians as they aimed their arrows at him. For an instant Cass allowed the blade to hover in the air before he strained every sinew to bring it down.

Then the hissing began to encircle both men, the man standing and the man on the ground.

The noise chilled Cass's soul as he brought the deadly weapon down. Then the arrows flew from all directions. There was only one target and Jacob Harvey Cass was it. The long arrows skewered the man so expertly the blade flew up into the air falling safely to the ground.

Bob Cooper watched in shock as the man he had hunted so long and so hard crumpled in a heap at his feet. His mission was over and yet, as he lay still unable to get his wind back, he wondered what would happen next to Juan and himself.

He did not have long to wonder as the small warriors led the tall Mexican towards him. There seemed to be countless hands helping him to his feet.

'You OK, *amigo*?' Cortez asked, placing a hand upon the shoulder of his friend.

Cooper felt the small warriors leading them towards the tunnel as he answered, 'So far, Juan. So far.'

Within the hour they were back at their horses in the canyon beyond the tunnel. The Seri were gone as quickly as they had appeared. The two men sat in their saddles wondering if what had occurred was truly reality or a shared dream.

'They've gone,' Cortez said, gathering up his loose reins as he spurred his horse forward.

Cooper followed. 'Why didn't they kill us like

151

they did the renegades, Juan?'

Juan Cortez shrugged as they increased their speed along the narrow valley. 'Maybe they understood.'

'Understood?' Cooper puzzled.

'Maybe they just understood, *amigo.*'

Whatever the reason for their release, neither man was about to complain. They were headed back towards the long trail that had brought them here. It would take a long time and they would meet Rosa and Don Jose Maldova along the way. Sometimes savages are not the ones wearing the war paint, they concluded.

FINALE

Bob Cooper led his horse from the stable within the courtyard of the Cortez *hacienda* across towards the large whitewashed house and all its glory. His eyes had never seen such a place before and it troubled him to think of how he had once lived. His home in Montana had been nothing more than a small dwelling made from slabs of dried sod and some split tree trunks. Mud had held it all together. The roof had been covered in turf and grass grew there. That was all he had managed to provide for his late wife and child. A slab of mud.

He stood beside the horse and checked that his saddle was well and truly secure. The horse drank from the welcoming trough as Cooper moved around it examining all the bits and pieces of tack. His was a strange mood and he had never before felt as he did this sunny new day. For the first time in two years he had nobody to chase. Nobody to hunt. Nobody to hate. It was indeed a new page in a new book, blank and devoid of anything recognizable. Hatred and vengeance had been the spurs that had driven him on his long quest. The thought of finding the men who had destroyed his life by taking away those he loved, had suddenly gone. He had nothing to hate any longer. His was now a life lacking any direction. It suddenly occurred to him as he moved around to his horse's bridle that he had nowhere to go any longer. The trail had ended. His mission was completed.

Bob Cooper could not say that he was happy at knowing the men who had killed his little family were dead; he had always thought it would make him happy and yet it did not. He could not say that he felt good at their deaths, he did not. All that seemed to fill him was an empty void where once his soul had been.

Was this the way it was supposed to feel?

Was this how it was meant to be?

He still wondered why the Indians had saved his life and released him and Juan. Had they truly known that he was not as evil as the men he had hunted? How could they have known that he was on a crusade?

He found himself staring around the courtyard and liking what he saw. This was a place that had a lot of things going for it and the main thing was love. He could see that this place had been created out of nothing and moulded together with the passion of people who loved it.

They had built something truly wonderful out here in the wilderness. They had created a heaven in an otherwise hostile environment.

Cooper sat on the edge of the trough and sighed to himself. It was early. Really early. Even the rooster was still asleep over at the henhouse. He had intended to simply mount up and light out of this place and here he was sitting on the trough feeling the water lapping at his jeans as his horse drank.

This was such a welcoming place that he wondered why he wanted to ride away, if indeed he did.

'Where you going, Cooper?' The sweet tones of Rosa Cortez filled his mind as he listened to her small feet coming closer to him. He turned and studied her. 'Why are you saddled up, my big strong one?'

Cooper rose to his feet as she came close. 'Miss Rosa.'

'I ask you the question, Cooper.' She stood below him looking up into his face as the first rays of daylight crept across the red-tiled roof tops.

'I'm heading out,' Cooper heard himself saying.

She seemed to suddenly look sad. 'You leave?'

'Yeah. I'm heading back north.'

'Why?' She stepped closer. Now she was so close that her body touched his.

'I have to return to Montana,' Cooper drawled, feeling her warm body touching his. It made the small hairs on the back of his neck tingle.

'You not want to stay with Rosa and Juan?' Rosa's face looked as if it were about to burst into tears as she fluttered her long black lashes at him.

Cooper stared down at her small young face. Such a beautiful face. She had only just reached adulthood and he felt as if he had been grown all his life. 'I like you and your brother and I owe you a lot but—'

'What is wrong my tall one?' She reached up and touched his cheek. He had tried not to look into her eyes, her large beautiful eyes, but had failed. Once his eyes met hers he felt his spine turn to jelly.

'I ought to go, Rosa,' he started. 'I'm too old for you and you deserve better.'

'You are not old, Cooper.' Her smile flashed at him. 'You are a man who has been hurt. Like my brother Juan was once hurt, but he is now better. You will get better. It takes a while to start living again.'

'I gotta go.' Cooper somehow managed to turn away from her and grabbed his reins. Then he felt her arms around him. Such strong arms for a small female. He turned and stared at her again.

'Stay, *amigo*.' The deep voice of Juan Cortez

boomed out from the darkness of the *hacienda* causing Cooper to look up. The tall Mexican stood with a cigar in his teeth and a glass of sherry in his raised hand. 'Stay and make my little Rosa happy. It might make you happy also.'

Cooper watched as the smiling man turned and walked back into the house not waiting for arguments.

'See?' Rosa grinned. 'You have the permission of my very old brother not only to stay but to marry me.'

'Marry you?' Cooper's jaw fell. 'He didn't say nothing about me marrying you, Rosa.'

She pointed a small finger at the blushing man. 'He say to make me happy. That is the same thing.'

Cooper pushed his hat back until it rested on the crown of his head. 'Wait on here just a darn minute, Rosa.'

Jumping up she grabbed his shoulders and pulled him forward until their lips met. The kiss was long and warm. At first Cooper tried to resist, but then he felt himself melting into her as her mouth consumed his every objection. When the kiss ended she stood smiling and he stood dazed.

'Well?' She beamed at him with a face that did not usually take to strangers. 'Will you stay and marry your Rosa?'

Cooper held the cantle of his saddle with one

hand whilst he toyed with his reins with the other.

'Well?' Rosa shouted, both fists clenched.

Bob Cooper started to smile and then he let go of the reins and took his hand off his saddle. He started to move toward her as his grin grew broader.

'What is your answer, my tall one?' Rosa asked, as he stepped before her.

Cooper did not answer. He lifted her off the ground and pulled her close, so close that each could feel the other's heart beating. The first page of his new book was starting to be written at long last, he thought. 'Do you know anyone who'll unsaddle my horse, ma'am?'